I0643425

Rachel Carew

Tangled

A Novel

Rachel Carew

Tangled
A Novel

ISBN/EAN: 9783337002527

Printed in Europe, USA, Canada, Australia, Japan

Cover: Foto ©Andreas Hilbeck / pixelio.de

More available books at **www.hansebooks.com**

TANGLED.

A NOVEL.

BY

RACHEL CAREW.

————

CHICAGO:
S. C. GRIGGS AND COMPANY.
1877.

KNIGHT & LEONARD, PRINTERS, CHICAGO.

TO

SIDNEY DAYRE

THIS STORY IS

AFFECTIONATELY DEDICATED.

TANGLED.

CHAPTER I.

INTRODUCTION.

A PAIR of shapely feet encased in embroidered
velvet slippers rests on the window-sill. The
greater part of the owner's conformation is obscured
by a cloud of tobacco smoke, but a kindly breeze parting the veil reveals, many degrees lower than the feet,
the figure of a very handsome, rather pale and altogether indolent-looking young gentleman, stretched
comfortably in an easy-chair. Does the attitude explain sufficiently his nationality, or is it necessary to
say that he is an American?

Although it is a July afternoon, Lawrence Conway
wraps his comely members in a thick, soft dressing-
gown and feels none too warm. Mr. Conway, having
nothing to do, has come to the conclusion that he is
an invalid. This decision was brought about in a

7

great measure by his anxious mother, who, hearing the family physician hint vaguely that young Conway's frequent headaches might develop into something serious if allowed to continue, took fright, and induced her beloved son to forego the gaieties and dissipations of Parisian life for a time, and try the effect of a highly recommended course of mineral baths in Switzerland.

Thus it came about that we find Lawrence ensconced in a handsome apartment in the *Grand Hôtel des Salines,* a mile from the picturesque little village of Bex. Presently the cigar stump goes flying out of the window, the feet come down with celerity, and our hero betakes himself to pacing the room in short, quick steps, angrily gnawing the ends of his tawny, drooping mustache.

"What a fool I was to let mother's fidgety notions banish me to this howling wilderness. I've been here three days, but three months could not have dragged themselves away any slower. Nothing to do but to take country walks, which is detestable when one has to go alone. No society but a ghastly array of old frights in various stages of decay, real and imaginary. These invalids everywhere are very depressing to one's spirits — a very Hercules would feel himself getting weak and ailing in their presence, from the force of example. A fellow can't walk in the grounds without tripping up on crutches, or getting his legs run over by invalid chairs. I stretch myself on a bench for a smoke, when just as I am beginning to dream myself back into civilization again, up totters an old lady, with her maid bearing rugs and shawls. She looks wistfully at my bench, although there are a dozen vacant ones to be had, and I have to hop up, expressing my indifference to repose, and help arrange the old lady in her shawls and wraps in the place where I had been so comfortable.

"The stray dozen or so of people who seem to enjoy themselves don't speak English. My bad French would only annoy them, so here I am, one of the most desolate fellows on the face of the earth. I can't even whistle to lighten my solitude, it wakes a bilious baby next door.

"Doctor Bernard — confound him!—might as well have recommended me to my grave, as to this dolorous retreat. The place is a paradise in situation and surroundings, but, infested with a hundred or so invalids who talk of nothing but their symptoms, what place could help being dreary? And I am bound to stay six weeks longer at least. Ye Gods! can a fellow live through it?"

In this despondent current flow the meditations of

Mr. Conway, till his attention is aroused by the grating of wheels on the gravel below.

"There is the omnibus with another load of victims. Judging by the amount of luggage they bring, the deluded beings have committed themselves for a long time. There are no crutches on top this time — that looks encouraging."

He watches with indifference the exit of a nurse-maid carrying one whining child and dragging another after her. She is followed by the anxious mamma, a prey to small bags and bundles of various sorts. An angular spinster emerges, and in excited French, spoken with a strong English accent, demands the instant restoration of the bath-tub to her tender care, which, aloft on the omnibus, contains all her worldly goods. Next come two portly gentlemen of uninteresting appearance.

At this point Lawrence begins to tire of the inspection and is turning away, when a glimpse of the next passenger through the omnibus window arrests him.

"By Jove, what a pretty girl!"

He shields himself from observation behind the half-drawn blind, and watches the movements of the young lady who has awakened his interest. She is very pretty; soft, baby-like curls about her forehead, in lovely contrast to the velvety brown eyes; a delicate complexion, a graceful figure shown to perfection in the closely-fitting dark blue dress, and a most charming little foot and ankle temptingly displayed when she alights from the omnibus. She is accompanied by a gentle-looking, white-haired old lady, whom Lawrence rightly guesses to be her mother.

"Mamma, dear, tell the man which is our luggage, while I go and ask about the Evans party," the younger lady said, quickly disappearing, leaving her mother to follow at her leisure.

Lawrence emerged from behind the blind.

"English," he mused; "and neither of them seem to be suffering from anything. I hope they are going to stay. An hour yet till dinner; of course they will come to the *table d'hôte*."

Mr. Conway, noted among his friends for good taste in dress, bestowed, on this particular evening, unusual care on his toilette. Could his mother have seen him as he walked up and down the terrace waiting for the gong to sound, with an unusual flush on his cheeks and sparkle in his dark eyes, she might have quieted her uneasiness for his bodily welfare, and felt justly proud of her handsome son.

Lawrence Conway was not always of the peevish,

unmanly temperament which these pages would so
far imply. Among his own friends he was admired
and looked up to as the embodiment of all that was
witty, intelligent and fascinating; and no feast or
entertainment of any kind was considered complete
unless graced by the presence of Lawrence Conway.
But to the world at large, outside the circle of his
tried friends and companions, Lawrence presented a
reserved if not altogether cold exterior. He had
spent the past few years in wandering from place to
place on the continent of Europe, sometimes with his
mother, but oftener forming one of a merry party of
tourists of almost all nations except French, and
herein lay the chief reason of his present unhappiness.
All their communication among each other had been
in English or German, and during Lawrence's stay
in Paris, and everywhere else in Europe, he had made
the fatal mistake of depending on some friend for
whatever French conversation was necessary; and
beyond a few every-day phrases and words that would
procure him food, lodging and railway tickets, he
knew nothing of the language. Consequently when
his health gave way a little, and he found himself
spirited away from all those whose society he enjoyed,
and dropped among a crowd of strangers speaking
an unknown tongue, he felt the desolation of dark-

ness fall upon him, and took a grim kind of pleasure
in exaggerating the trials of his situation.

If Mr. Conway, after completing his toilette, had
continued to gaze out of the window, he might have
witnessed, an hour later, another arrival.

Not the omnibus this time, but a covered carriage,
with no luggage on the top. Two ladies and a boy
of fourteen were the occupants. As they alighted,
the younger of the two ladies exclaimed: "It seems
like home to be here again, doesn't it, mamma?"

"Yes," answered the other lady. "What a pity
it is we have to start off again to-morrow."

"You needn't go unless you want to," said the
boy. "I would rather go alone."

"But you could not go alone, Jack, you know
very well. Winnie, ask who are among the new
arrivals,— though I suppose it is hardly time for
the Franklands yet."

"Have there been any English arrivals to-day, or
were there any yesterday?" the young lady asked
of one of the servants.

"Mademoiselle will perhaps have the goodness to
inform herself by a glance at the strangers list,"
answered the man, opening a much begilded book
for her inspection.

"Oh, mamma, the Franklands are here! See, there

are their names. How delightful! Show us their rooms directly, please. Come, mamma, and see them. Come, Jack, we haven't much time."

The party ran quickly upstairs, and during their absence our patient reader must kindly accept a short explanation.

Mrs. Evans, with her daughter Winnie, and Jack, her son, had been spending the summer at the *Hôtel des Salines*. Contrary to the opinion of our friend, Lawrence Conway, they had found the place charming. Master Jack, at the opening of our story, was on the eve of departure for a school in Germany, on which journey his mother and sister were to accompany him the following day. For the benefit of this young gentleman the family had been to Chamonix, and it was from this excursion that they had returned the evening of the arrival of Mrs. Frankland and her daughter. It is, perhaps, needless to mention that the latter were the ladies whose advent in the omnibus was watched and approved by Mr. Conway.

The two families were on intimate terms of friendship, and it was at the urgent request of Mrs. Evans and Winnie that the Franklands had come to spend a few weeks at the *Hôtel des Salines*.

The young ladies were heart-broken at the thought

of separating again so soon, but Mrs. Evans hoped to return from Germany in a fortnight, at least, and then they could make up for lost time.

The temporary reunion of this friendly party brings up so many interesting topics of conversation that they decide to dine *en famille* in their own rooms. The carefully arrayed Mr. Conway takes his place at the *table d'hôte* and anxiously waits the arrival of the new guests—and waits in vain. For some time the two vacant chairs opposite him excite delusive hopes in his manly bosom, but as time wears on and they continue unoccupied, and as no pretty girl with yellow hair is visible elsewhere in the room (there are yellow-haired girls, but in no other way resembling his charmer), he devours the remainder of his dinner in silent, gloomy disgust.

CHAPTER II.

IN WHICH MISS FRANKLAND'S INTEREST IS AWAKENED.

THE following morning dawns bright and beautiful as the preceding day. Mr. Conway saunters out on his balcony, with much the usual look of discontent on his handsome face; but as his roving eye takes in the scene around him, that he had called a "howling wilderness" the evening before, an involuntary exclamation of pleasure bursts from him.

On one side stretches the irregular chain of the Vaudois Alps, many showing their ragged tops far above the fleecy, low-lying clouds; a range of forest-grown, or grassy, cultivated hills,— terminated on one side by the snow-crowned peak of the *Dent du Midi*, on the other by the rugged *Dent de Morcles*, both reflecting their vast heads in the Rhone, that winds beneath,— shuts in completely that part of the Rhone valley in which Bex is situated.

The immediate surroundings of the *Hôtel des Salines* are picturesque almost beyond description,— a

vast stretch of cultivated park, arranged according
to the English manner of landscape gardening, with
velvet-like turf, shady walks, a lake, myriads of rare
flowers and fruits, and further ornamented with statues, fountains and grottoes, and everything that
makes a summer sojourn delightful.

The subtle beauty of the scene stole over Lawrence, and with heart-felt admiration he exclaimed:

"By Jove! this is fine.   I don't believe I realized
how beautiful it was before.   They say people never
appreciate Alpine grandeur at first sight.   It grows
on them the more they see of it, and the longer they
stay among these mountains the harder it is to leave
them.   I suppose that is the reason the Swiss are so
strongly attached to their country, and are so troubled with *heim-weh* when they leave it."

Lawrence, as he continues to gaze about him,
whistles a verse of *"Herz, mein Herz, warum so
traurig?"*   He is on the balcony, so it does not dis-
turb the sick baby.

"That. bit of ruined tower, over on the hill in
front, looks attractive; my 'constitutional' this
morning shall be exploring it.   A fellow might
manage to kill time here very comfortably, if he
only had some one to go about with."

Lawrence comes in from the balcony, and after a

delicate breakfast, consisting of chocolate, fresh rolls and honey, daintily served in his sitting-room, he sallies forth to visit the ruins of the *Tour de Douin*.

Up another flight of stairs Miss Winnie Evans is skimming through the corridors with winged feet. She must be off in a few hours, and in that time has many preparations to make and much gossip to discuss with Emily Frankland. She taps at the door of her friend's room, calling:

"Come, Emily, dear, you must give me an hour in the grounds before I go. It is a perfectly lovely morning,— it is wicked to stay in the house."

"I have been waiting for you half an hour, Winnie," answered Emily, joining her friend, and in five minutes more the two girls were walking, arm-in-arm, down one of the shady, fragrant avenues.

Beautiful Emily, with her shell-like complexion and golden hair, and the impish little brown-eyed gypsy, Winnie, add in no small degree to the beauty of that bright summer morning.

"What sort of people are there in the hotel now, Winnie?"

"Not a very interesting lot at present,— mostly invalids, so far as I know. I have been away nearly a week, you know, and there may be new-comers; but I saw very few unfamiliar faces at the breakfast table this morning,—what few I saw, looked like bores."

"How glad I am I didn't breakfast downstairs!"

"You foolish child! Do you suppose I would call your pretty face 'unfamiliar'?"

"You might in this place."

"But I wouldn't anywhere. But to return to the subject in hand. There is a very nice party of seven coming in a fortnight, about the time we come back. Until then you will find it stupid, I am afraid."

"Which will break up the stupidity, you or the party of seven?"

"Both, I hope. I think three rather nice-looking Italian girls are still here; also a German officer, whom you can classify for yourself; and a yellow-haired Scotchman, whom we always call 'the fair one with golden locks.' He is so absurdly conceited there is no enduring him. Then there is a very nice Russian family, but the grown-up son and daughters are still at Chamouix. Let me think—who else is there? I fairly adore a lovely girl in the room next to mine, but she is quite blind, poor thing, and of course can't be depended on much as a companion."

"So far, your list shows a great scarcity of beaux, Winnie."

"Oh, it is always so; nice men hardly ever come

to a quiet, dull place like this, unless they are ill, and then they are too abominably cross to be of any use. I wonder if the three Oxford students are still here — familiarly known as the 'three little kittens.' They were perfectly delightful, and ——"

"Winnie, I beg your pardon for interrupting, but what does that man over there mean by lifting his hat to every one of those ducks waddling past? There he goes again, was ever anything so perfectly ridiculous!"

"Oh, how could I have forgotten to tell you about Darwin!" Winnie exclaimed. "It is a long history, though very little known among the people here. I shall hardly have time to tell you before ——"

"Do begin, never mind preliminaries."

"He is a Polish count, and his real name is Victor de Lemanski; but I am principled against calling people by their right names, when I can find any that suit them better. He is very rich, quite young, and would be very attractive if his poor wits were not all on the rampage. So far, his history is interesting, is it not? But I am afraid you will find the rest too ridiculous even to pity him."

"Go on, dear, I shall be the best judge of that."

"He is quite insane, but also perfectly harmless. He believes that every beast, bird and fish is some

human being transformed,— except parrots, which he
detests. He declares they must have been devils in
their former state; for if otherwise, they, having the
power of speech, would discourse about their former
existence; but as they say nothing about it, the in-
ference is that they were devils, and are ashamed of
the fact. Ducks, geese and pigeons he thinks were
once beautiful young ladies ———"

"Not very complimentary to the sex, is it?"

"No, that's what I thought. So whenever he sees
any of these birds he lifts his hat, and bows with
unusual deference, believing that if he omitted these
politenesses, they would be as much offended as if
they still had their human forms."

"So that is the reason why he takes his hat off to
the ducks. Do tell me something more about the
extraordinary creature. Has he been here all summer,—or what interests me more, is he going to
stay long?"

"Oh yes. You will have plenty of time to take
note of his peculiarities for yourself. But remember,
people don't talk about him much, out of respect to
his mother."

"Is his mother here?"

"No, not at present; they have to send for her
sometimes when her son gets very unmanageable.

She has more power over him, of course, than any one else."

"Is he often violent?"

"No, but he gets such queer ideas about himself,— turns himself into a whole menagerie, mentally."

"The poor fellow!"

"Then when his spirit comes back among human beings again, it does not always return to his own person, and he imagines himself somebody else."

"What a pity he could not imagine he was a very sensible person, and keep up the delusion always."

"He is too much of a weather-cock for that. The poor creature keeps himself so uncomfortable with his notions; he never will ride or drive, because he says it is an indignity offered to a human being in the form of the horse. It is too ridiculous to see him nodding and smiling to all the cats and dogs about the place. One day I heard him reading aloud a long article on the merits of blue glass, to a lame donkey tethered over in that meadow."

"Can people expect these very strange demonstrations at all times?"

"One can never be sure of him. He came into the drawing-room one evening with some bits of lace and tumbled artificial flowers stuck in his hair; he carried a basket on his arm scrawled over with names of Swiss villages, and decorated with dabs of red flannel,—an eccentric representation of the style of basket that many English ladies admire.   It contained a ball of red yarn and a boot buttoner, he sat down on a hard, uncomfortable chair, took out the yarn and hook and commenced to crochet.   From his conversation and manners we all guessed directly that he thought himself the painfully prim little English governess, who is here with some Russian children."

"Was the governess herself in the room?"

"Yes, but she either did not recognize herself, or else would not admit the resemblance."

"Perhaps this Pole used to be an actor and went crazy with enthusiasm."

"No he didn't; he's been cracked all his life."

"But why do they let him make a spectacle of himself before strangers?"

"He is very cunning about escaping from his keepers when an insane fit comes on, but I believe they are more vigilant now; he has not done anything very amiss during the past two or three weeks.   One of the last things he did was to frighten the same little English governess nearly out of her wits one night.   A little past midnight a weird, ghostly sound was heard issuing from a tree near her window.   It was something between a bark and a groan, and whether human or otherwise, no one could make out. After much poking and stirring up with a long stick, the mystery was discovered to be Darwin, perched on one of the higher branches. He declared he was an owl, and would have sat there hooting and groaning all night, if some thoughtful individual had not aimed a gun at him and frightened him down."

"But I should think the boarders would rebel against having such an uncomfortable person about."

"His friends tried putting him into an asylum, but the confinement made him so much worse he had to be taken away."

"But there are private asylums where he could stay quite comfortably."

"That has been tried, too; but when his wandering fit wears off—and it never lasts very long—he guesses directly if he is being kept in a kind of bondage, and it makes him low-spirited and miserable. He likes to be among a crowd of people, and this is the quietest place they can find where he is content to stay."

"Perhaps, this being a water-cure for all kinds of ailments, they take lunatics as a matter of course."

"I hardly think that, for his mother pays the pro-

prietor of the hotel a fabulous sum for letting him
spend the summer here."

"He must be a dreadful grief to his mother."

"No one knows how much she suffers. He is an
only son, too. Out of pity to the mother no one
complains of him, as in that case he would have to
be sent away."

"Does she come to visit him often?"

"I have seen her once,—a tall, graceful woman,
with such a sad, beautiful face! Her hair is quite
white, but in spite of it, with her slender figure and
pure clear complexion, she does not look even middle-
aged."

"Why, poor Darwin, from this distance, looks as
if he might be five and twenty, at least."

"He looks older than he is."

"You seem to have all his history on your fingers'
ends, Winnie; can it be possible you have lost your
heart to this crazy count?"

"No, it is not so bad as that, but he is almost
irresistible in some of his clear moments."

"Is he often rational?"

"Sometimes for weeks together he is quite sensible,
and strangers only think him a quiet, reserved young
man. He is always quite harmless; and they say if
one humors his ideas of transformation, and induces

him to talk on the subject, he shows a good deal of quaint eloquence and distorted intelligence."

"I suppose you have drawn him out on his favorite theme many times, Winnie."

"Oh dear no! I should be frightened to death if I drew eloquence out of anybody; I wouldn't know how to receive or stop it."

"You absurd little goose! But go on, dear; tell me all you know about Darwin,— he seems to be the most interesting character about the place."

"He sees a resemblance to some animal in almost every person he meets, and believes that when people disappear from his neighborhood they have gone to assume the shapes of the animals they are most like. This gives him a rather unpleasant habit of staring fixedly at a new-comer for several minutes, after which he growls, barks, crows or mews, according as his or her appearance suggests."

"How he must take the conceit out of people!"

"But he sometimes finds very flattering resemblances. There was a young lady here, early in the summer, who sang very well, and he always called her Mademoiselle Nilsson, or the Swedish Nightingale."

"What has he decided you are most like, Winnie?"

"Oh, I never dared investigate too closely. 'Where ignorance is bliss,' you know."

"Does he speak French?"

"Yes, and English too, like a native."

"How could such a poor, rattle-brained fellow learn different languages?"

"I suppose he picked them up when he was a baby. His mother is English, so it is not strange that he knows that language. During one of his sensible fits one would take him for an ordinary English tourist. I take a deep interest in Darwin, Emily, and while I am gone I want you to treat him as kindly as you safely can."

"I will, dear. I promise you to do my best to keep him cheerful in your absence. I will make an effort to amuse him whenever he falls in my way; I will take him wherever we go, and smile on him ——"

"If you do all that you will certainly repent it. I only meant that you were not to let him see that you thought him different from other people. He is very susceptible to notice and attentions, and if you smiled on him once he would never forget it, and would follow you about like a dog for the rest of your stay. Then, when his next crazy fit came on, you would be the one to suffer. Seriously, you must be rather cold and reserved toward him, Emily; only don't ignore and neglect him as the other people do."

"It would be better not to encounter him at all;

he seems to be turning out a very uncomfortable sort of person."

"It will be impossible to avoid him, I think, for his place at table is just opposite yours."

"What shall I do if the dreadful monster inclines to be friendly?"

"Answer him politely, but briefly as possible. It requires some tact to talk to him so that he shall see you neither treat him differently from other people, nor are disposed to make a companion of him. I think it does him good to talk to him a little, sometimes, as if he were like his fellow-beings. The best way, in his presence, is to make yourself out a very common-place, thick-headed young person, so he will neither fall in love with you nor think you a dragon. This *rôle* was not difficult for me; you will find it more troublesome, Emily, as you have too many wits to hide them under a bushel."

"I never knew you to be so complimentary before, Winnie; what has come over you?"

"I suppose it is because I am going away, and want to leave a good impression. But all this time, Emily, you have not had more than a glimpse of Darwin."

"Let us make haste and overtake him."

"No, that wouldn't do; you must not attract his attention in that way at the very first, he would be sure to remember you.   We can skirt around this little path and meet him face to face in a most natural way on the avenue; then you can raise your eyes once and get a good look at him, and then we will walk on as if we had seen nothing."

The little footpath chosen by the girls was only used as a short-cut through the trees, furtively adopted by the peasant boys who brought goat's milk to the hotel, and was, consequently, in very indifferent order for pedestrians in general.   After a scramble of five minutes, over gnarled roots, slippery pine-needles and moss, the two young ladies emerged on the avenue, some distance farther on than where they had been walking before.

"Oh, how very vexatious!" exclaimed Winnie; "there comes his attendant, and he is going to take him back to the house.   They are actually turning their backs on us as we were almost on them.   We must give up the chase, I suppose."

"But I shall of course recognize him from what you have told me."

"Oh yes, you can't mistake him; a tall, handsome fellow, with a thick mustache and dark eyes; rather pale and delicate-looking, of course.   In fact he is the only man of that description about the place, so you will have no trouble in knowing him again; but

I wanted to show him to you, as well as tell you about him, and perhaps I might have introduced him to you, if he had been sufficiently sensible."

"You will be a good subject for conversation with Darwin while you are gone, Winnie."

"Very likely he will have forgotten all about me when you mention my name."

"Do you think so? If there are no other excitements here, I shall take a great interest in the study of this poor fellow."

"The study may begin at dinner, if you like, for he must be quite rational now, or they would not let him walk about alone,—the keeper joining him did not prove that anything was wrong. But remember, Emily dear, my solemn warning: do not gush over him! be calm, and stately, and severe, as you can be when you choose, and you will not have much to apprehend. He will of course fall in love with you, because you are so pretty, so you will have to exert yourself to frighten him into a comfortable state of meekness and unobtrusiveness."

"Winnie, what a shame you are off again just as we come! I don't realize yet that you are going. You must not be gone long."

"You may be sure I won't, darling. Remember all we talked about last night, and I will——

"But there comes Jack, waving an umbrella and looking fierce and important. That means we are to set off."

"Winnie, it is just like you to go straggling about the place when there are a heap of things to do. I have been tying strings and locking trunks all the morning."

"What else are boys good for, I should like to know. I got up early and did everything I had to do while you were asleep, like the lazy fellow you are."

"Lazy, is it?—after the way I have been on the trot for you this morning;" and Jack began an affecting account of his fatiguing search for his sister, to which that young lady listened unmoved.

"But mother will go without us if we don't go back," he added, with the air of an officious martyr, escorting the young ladies to where a trunk-laden carriage was standing.

Many friends had assembled to watch the start, and after a deluge of farewell words and caresses, the Evans family drove away on their first stage toward the beautiful Rhine-land.

Miss Winnie, owing to her recent absence, was mistaken regarding the present docility of the unfortunate Count Lemanski. His latest freak had

developed itself only two days before, and he was
more refractory than he had been for many weeks.

Nothing could shake his belief that he was a St.
Bernard dog, and he had been going about for a day
or two with a small flask of brandy tied around his
neck, which he offered on all-fours to anyone who
appeared to him to be in need of refreshment.

This in itself was not a bad idea, had he carried
the representation no further; but as he had tried on
one occasion, at the *table d'hôte*, to eat and drink
after the manner of all dogs, and afterward had
betaken himself to barking vociferously, it was concluded necessary to put him under restraint. He
was allowed to walk a little every morning in a re-
mote part of the grounds, and it was to bring him
in from this walk that the attendant met him on
the morning of Miss Evans'. departure.

That night the poor young man became so violent
that it was decided to keep him a close prisoner in
his own rooms till the paroxysm should wear off, and
he should be collected enough to appear in public
again. An improvement could always be expected
in the course of a week or ten days, after which he
was usually, for many days together, gentle as a lamb.

The melancholy history of this young man was
kept as much as possible from the knowledge of the

ordinary guests at the *Hôtel des Salines,* and it was
only to people there for many weeks at a time that
his sad story was known.   He was allowed to appear in public only when apparently sane; and when
during his wandering moments he, on rare occasions,
escaped the vigilance of his guards and made himself ridiculous, people charitably hushed up the oc-
currence or forgot it.   Among the constantly shifting
crowds at the hotel there were few who had ever heard
of Count Lemanski, so the poor fellow's shadowy existence was little the subject of comment.

Miss Evans, as one of the longest residents at the
hotel, had had ample opportunity to learn and interest herself in the poor lunatic's history, but even
she rarely discussed the subject with strangers.

CHAPTER III.

OUR HERO LOSES HIS IDENTITY.

WITH a muffled but penetrating grumbling of the gong the guests of the *Grand Hôtel des Salines* are apprised that dinner is served, and the doors of the handsome dining-rooms are thrown wide open, revealing a most inviting scene within. Everything glistens and shines, from the polished mosaic floor to the delicately frescoed ceilings. The walls, formed of artistically painted panels alternating with gilded mirrors reaching from floor to ceiling, reflect a brilliant array of silver, crystal, and snowy linen. A profusion of flowers everywhere — on the tables and in great banks of bloom at the end windows. Gleaming white statues peer out of groves of tropical plants, and a cunningly contrived fountain keeps the air refreshingly cool. Black-robed servants stand silent and immovable as the marble figures about them, till the stream of guests beginning to pour in awakes this enchanted palace to life and activity.

The seven o'clock dinner hour is the great event of the day at the *Hôtel des Salines*. The confirmed

invalids dine earlier, so the company that assembles
at the late dinner is generally cheerful and animated.

Russians predominate among the guests, and make
themselves most noticeable by their quick, graceful
gestures, while their brilliant conversation never fails
to enliven the dullest assemblage. There are a few
comfortable looking German matrons, with their shy,
romance-loving daughters, who leave most of the
talking to be done by their husbands and brothers;
then comes a plentiful sprinkling of English tourists of both sexes — sun-burnt, weary and worn-look-
ing with their hard mountain exercise, but triumphant and happy at having one less steep ascent to
climb. They offer a strong contrast to the graceful, talkative, tastefully dressed French ladies beside
them. Next on the list are a bevy of pretty American girls, with the qualities of flirting and dressing
developed to perfection. All these are dotted about
among a miscellaneous crowd of people, old and
young, bearing a general resemblance to each other,
caused by a state of semi-invalidism, and a conse-
quent indifference to aiming at any distinction in
dress or manners.

Mrs. Frankland and her daughter were among the
first who entered the room. Their chairs were placed
at some distance from the other guests, owing to a

gap at the table caused by the absence of a large party on an excursion in the neighborhood. There was, however, one vacant place opposite them, and Emily was eagerly watching for its occupant. But no one appeared as course after course of the bountiful repast came and went, till at last, as she had given up all hope of seeing the object of her interest that day, the door of the *salle-à-manger* reopened and our friend, Lawrence Conway, entered the room.

"There he is, mamma!" Emily exclaimed, in an undertone.

"Who, my dear? You seem quite excited."

"Why, the crazy Count, of course. Brown mustache, pale complexion, dark eyes,—Winnie's description exactly."

"Don't look at him, my dear,—he seems to be coming this way."

"You never would suppose that well-dressed, handsome fellow to be a lunatic, would you, mamma? He's going to sit opposite us. I'm so glad,—oh, I wish he wouldn't, I shall be frightened to death if he speaks!"

"Emily, I repeat Winnie's warning—you must not speak to him any more than the barest civility demands," whispered Mrs. Frankland, hastily. "I do wish the young man's place was somewhere else."

Handsome Lawrence Conway, with very different ideas coursing through his brain, put all his soul into the graceful bow made before taking his seat, and found himself installed opposite the two ladies with extreme satisfaction.

"I thought the fair recluse would appear among us soon," he mused. "Pretty girls are not generally averse to being looked at. What a lovely sprite she is! Prettier, if possible, with her hat off than when I saw her first. I wonder if she is bashful. She doesn't look so. Had I better speak to her first, being the longest resident here, or will either of them open the conversation?—women are never backward where talking is to be done. I would like to ask them such a lot of questions about how long they are going to stay and what they want to see—but I must not let them think me rude and inquisitive on the first interview. Life here would have quite an object if these ladies would stay. Of course they would make trips and excursions, and would want some escort,—I might, perhaps, be that escort."

Emily's reverie was much more unsatisfactory:—"What a treasure this man might be!" she thought, "so high-bred looking; such beautiful eyes, and such perfect manners. Oh dear, why is he not like

other men? But I suppose if he had his wits, in
addition to his other charms, he would be spoiled
by flattery. So, perhaps, it is just as well that most
of his screws are loose. Winnie's legacy is all that
can be desired as to exterior;—what a pity appearances are so deceitful."

By this time Lawrence had come to the conclusion that neither of the ladies intended to address
him. Perhaps it was only his imagination, but they
seemed to avoid, as much as possible, even glancing
toward him. Once he caught the young lady's eye,
but she had instantly looked down, with an incomprehensible, half-frightened expression on her pretty
face. The mother and daughter spoke occasionally
to each other on every-day subjects, but no remark
of theirs offered the least opportunity for Lawrence
to answer.

But he was not in the least abashed, and deter-
mined to open a conversation. He particularly
wished to say something out of the ordinary, but
nothing brilliant occurred to him. In drawing
toward him a dish of fruit, an orange rolled off,
upsetting his wine-glass and sending the contents
flying across the table toward Miss Frankland's
plate.

"I beg a thousand pardons!" exclaimed Lawrence,

blushing crimson at his own awkwardness. "I hope none of it has gone on your dress."

Emily, who saw the accident, but not the cause, answered, hurriedly, "It is nothing; pray don't mention it."

As the *garçon* was spreading a napkin over the deluged table-cloth, Emily said, in an undertone, to her mother:

"He is beginning to smash the dishes—what will he do next? Do you see how red his face is?"

"Don't be alarmed, my dear; I saw how the glass was broken—it was quite accidental."

Lawrence comforted himself with the fact that this slight accident had broken the silence between his *vis-à-vis* and himself; and for fear the ground gained should be lost again, he observed, addressing Emily:

"This is a charming situation for a hotel, is it not?"

"Very," was the response.

"Do you intend remaining long? I believe that is the proper thing to ask strangers on their arrival here."

"It is very uncertain how long we stay." (Pause.)

"She doesn't seem inclined to talk much," mused our hero. "I'll try the mother." (Aloud)—"There are some lovely walks in this neighborhood. I explored that ruin on the hill to the left, this morning. Do you know anything of its history,—possibly Bex, and its surroundings, are familiar to you?"

"No, this is our first visit in this locality."

"I suppose you are fond of walking?"

"Moderately so; we are not as great pedestrians as English people usually are."

As Lawrence poured himself out another glass of wine, he could not help thinking that neither his charmer nor her mother were brilliant in conversation.

"He is talking nonsense now, mamma," said Emily, softly,—"he never thought of going to that ruined tower, but was in the grounds all the morning."

While Miss Frankland appeared to be intently listening to a very animated conversation going on further down the table, Lawrence took the occasion to refresh himself with a good, comprehensive look at his fair neighbor.

"When I have a wife," he thought, "she shall always dress in white, with sprays of forget-me-not in her hair, and shall look like this girl, with big brown eyes and silky yellow hair. What lovely little hands she has!"

As Miss Frankland glanced toward him again, he asked:

"Do you recognize any old acquaintances among these people?"

"No, there is not one familiar face among them all," Emily answered, intently peeling a fig.

"Did you hear the music this afternoon? The band is unusually good for a place of this kind."

"No, we were not home in time."

"Have you much faith in the mineral waters here?"

"I have heard of a good many cures, so there must be something beneficial about them."

Lawrence thought perhaps if he were to remain silent, the young lady might introduce some topic on which she cared to talk; for certainly, so far, he had failed to interest her. But nothing was said, and the silence grew oppressive again.

"Is the girl a fool, or in a bad temper, or what the devil is the matter with her that she can't talk!" Lawrence ejaculates mentally.

Snubbing is a perfectly new experience to him, and he does not take it kindly. He feels an odd mixture of anger, admiration and disappointment, and bows, coldly and stiffly enough this time, as with a rustle and flutter of white frills and blue ribbons, and a dignified sweeping of black silk, the Franklands leave the table.

Our hero's reflections regarding them are not altogether complimentary, but their unapproachable manner has had the effect of doubling his interest.

"I have seen plenty of the reserve that English girls are supposed to possess, but I never before encountered such an icy specimen as this. She seemed astonished at my speaking to her at the *table d'hôte*, where everybody makes friends with his neighbor if he chooses. The golden-haired beauty looked something more than a bashful school-girl. I can't understand either of them; I wonder where they came from. It seems impossible to get anything out of them except by direct catechising, and that is unpleasant. I know I have no right to question them much; but if people want to keep themselves so mysterious, they should stay at home. Perhaps they have some trouble weighing on their minds,—but they do not wear mourning." And Mr. Conway stroked his mustache thoughtfully. "I must go and find Vera,—she appreciates and cares for me, if no one else does."

As Lawrence walked slowly down toward the croquet ground, a pretty little blue-eyed girl sprang forward to meet him, catching hold of his hands and swinging herself up into his arms, and then down to the ground again.

"Oh, Mr. Conway, I will so much say you something! So long I have waited for you."

"Speak out, Vera,—I'm all attention."

"I hate Miss Hammond, and I am going to dead her."

"What! kill your English governess! Then you would forget English, and could not be my little friend any more. You know I won't talk to you when you speak bad English, as you did yesterday."

"What did I say yesterday?"

"When old Mrs. Bradly asked you if your little brother was a delicate child, what did you say?"

"I said 'no, he is very wholesome.' That was not right—I remember what you told me. I will not more say so."

"But Miss Hammond,—what has she done?"

"You say it, so she may still live some more time; but she may not say bad, wicked things about my mamma."

"Why, what did she say?"

"She did say it was vulgar, and a long word I remember no more, for a ladies to smoke cigarettes. What does a Russian savage mean?"

"Nothing very bad."

"She said no lady wouldn't do it—only a Russian savage. My mamma is a lady, and she does smoke cigarettes. I hate that *affreuse* Miss Hammond!" cried Vera, stamping her little white-slippered foot on the gravel.

"Who did Miss Hammond say this to?"

"To another English miss."

"My dear child, she did not mean you to hear, and you must forget it. It was very wrong of her to say such things, but she did not mean any harm."

"Do you find it bad for to smoke cigarettes?"

"No, Vera, not for your mother,—she is Russian, and it is quite right for Russian ladies to do what is considered proper in their country. Miss Hammond should have remembered this."

"Oh! see how much I have marked my dress with strawberries!"

"You have,—you ought to wear dark clothes, and then you could be as much of a tom-boy as you like. Why are you always dressed in white, Vera?—white shoes, too?"

"Because I must."

"Why 'must'?—because your mother likes it?"

"No, because Our Lady likes it."

"What do you mean?"

"Do you not have little girls in your country, made *dédiées* — given to the Holy Mother of Jesus? I am that."

"Oh, you are dedicated to the Virgin,—is that it?"

"Yes, and so I must wear always white or blue colors till I am a big, long girl. Those colors please Our Lady, and she will be kind to children who wear them."

"And when you are grown up,—what then?"

"I then be dressed as a lady, like mamma, or go in a *couvent* and be a nun."

"Do you think you would like to be a nun?"

"I can't tell,—it is so many, many years till one be old."

"How old are you now?"

"I have seven years old."

"Do you wear all those white embroidered things in winter, too?"

"Yes; but I wear, too, white fur and warm things of wool; but everything,—bonnet, gloves, shoes,—all must be of white or of blue."

"I wonder if your mamma would have dedicated you to the Holy Mother if you had not been a white-skinned, golden-haired little thing to whom blue and white would be vastly becoming?"

"Now I not understand."

"It is just as well you didn't, my dear. But, Vera, you haven't told me your name to-day,—I must learn it one syllable at a time, till I remember it; tell me again."

" Veronica Alexandra von Kolatschewski."

"How did you ever grow up with such a long name?"

As Lawrence spoke, Vera's baby brother appeared, pushed in his carriage by a rosy-cheeked Norman girl, in a finely embroidered muslin cap, with gay plaid ribbons floating far below her waist, a spotless white apron and short petticoat revealing red stockings and slippers with large buckles.

The attention of the pretty maid was given more to a black-eyed young man engaged in trimming the turf borders than to her young charge, who had fallen asleep, and was in great danger of rolling out of his little basket carriage.

Vera sprang from Mr. Conway's side, and in a torrent of prettily spoken French gave the maid a sound scolding for her carelessness. The young woman received it with astonishing meekness, which proved Vera possessed of an authority far beyond her years; and straightening the sleepy baby she went solemnly on her way.

"Where did you learn so many languages, Vera?" resumed Lawrence.

"I don't know. In my home everybody speak

much languages. It is not *difficile*. My papa speak well eight."

"How many do you know?"

"Oh me! I know not yet many,— some French, German, some English, and Russian of course. I know Italian a few, but will learn better when I go to Italy next winter with my mamma."

"You don't learn out of books?"

"Oh no,— out of governesses and *bonnes*; and my mamma and papa speak not always the same language with me. You teach me much English, Mr. Conway."

"Do I, indeed?"

"Yes; Miss Hammond is abominable. I always talk awfully English with she, and with everybody but you."

"So I am a kind of angel in disguise if I make you take pains. I'm sure you don't know what that means."

"An angel in de skies,—yes, I understand. But you are not like one."

"Why not?"

"You don't dress naked, and sit always on a damp cloud."

"But I don't mean that kind of an angel."

"But I saw—oh *mon Dieu!*—so many in Paris, and they did all were like that."

"There are angels out of pictures, little girl."

"Is that pretty lady with a white dress and yellow hairs, who sits *vis-a-vis* you at dinner, a angel?"

"Why, what made you think of her, child?"

"Because why, I see her going over to the music. The band will going to be play. I must soon go to bed."

"Come, little one, we will go back together. When you are a big girl I will ask you to come to the concert with me. Will you come?"

"Yes, with *plaisir*. Will you wait for me to be a lady?"

"I'm sure I could not do better. But good-night now, child. There is your *bonne* looking for you. Pleasant dreams!"

"I will dream about you and the pretty lady,—you are both so nice," said Vera, giving Lawrence a parting kiss and hug.

Even for the quick, brilliant, pleasure-loving nation to which she belonged, Vera von Kolatschewski was a remarkably clever, intelligent child. Her short life had been mostly spent in following with her mother the fashionable world to its summer and winter haunts, so her education had begun at an unusually early age.

Lawrence took very little interest in most children,

but in his solitude at the *Hôtel des Salines* this bright little girl had taken a strong hold on his affections, and he found in her a very amusing companion.

After the departure of the child, Lawrence betook himself to the neighborhood of the band pavilion, and seating himself at a convenient distance from the music, prepared to take observations of the audience.

Mr. Conway had exaggerated the decrepit state of his fellow-boarders. Invalids there were, undoubtedly, but their number was well balanced by the gaily dressed, cheerful groups walking about or sitting near the pavilion. Lawrence watched their movements with idle indifference. The only person among the assembly, in whom he felt an interest, had given him the cold shoulder on their first interview. He saw her now,— this golden-haired beauty who had been so much in his mind of late,— promenading with an angular gentleman, whom she was apparently bewitching with her bright smiles and animated conversation.

"She seems to be able to talk to other men. There is none of the stiff English miss about her now. She will not even glance toward me. She saw me when she came in, but she won't look my way again for fear she will have to recognize me. Am I branded

as a scamp, that she has made a vow to avoid me?
I believe I am working myself into a bad temper
because a brown-eyed girl refuses to smile on me,
and favors a lanky Dutchman instead. This is what
comes of having nothing to do. I believe I will go
back to Paris, and report myself a wonderful case of
cure in a week's time."

Mr. Conway's meditations were of too gloomy a
character to be in keeping with the scene around
him. This fact struck him forcibly during the
second pause in the music, and with an angry shrug
of the shoulders he left the crowd of hollow pleasure-
seekers, and finished the evening on his balcony with
a cigar and the stars for company.

CHAPTER IV.

MR. CONWAY IS PERPLEXED.

EMILY was loitering about, the morning after the concert, picking up stray orange blossoms which had fallen from the boxed trees along the terrace. Mrs. Frankland was sitting near, on a rustic seat, working at an elaborate piece of English point lace.

"Mamma, don't you think we snubbed that poor fellow too much at dinner yesterday? I saw him flush up once, and look really annoyed because we didn't talk."

"No, Emily, I think we did perfectly right. It is much better to let him see from the very first that we mean to keep him at a distance. He evidently admires you; his glances told that plainly, without his persistent efforts to keep up a conversation he must have seen you were anxious to avoid. It was really a very unpleasant situation; I think we had better have our places at table changed."

"On no, mamma, that would be too marked!"

"Marked! My dear, you surely do not suppose

that a poor brainless fellow would notice the difference of such an arrangement?"

"I can't tell, of course, whether he would or not; but it is much better not to have our places changed. Mamma, are you going to sit here all the morning?"

"No, dear, only till I have worked round this corner. You take a ramble, if you like, and meet me here again in half an hour. How delicious this orange-scented air is!"

"Very well, mamma, if you won't come, I suppose I must go alone. If I meet with no adventures, I will be back in the course of an hour."

"Don't go far, and have nothing to say to that young Count, if you should meet him. Do you hear?"

"*Cela dépend*, mamma!" answered Emily, as she laughingly disappeared.

She was sweetly pretty as she fluttered away among the trees, her light, fluffy curls tied simply back with a blue ribbon, after the rustic, undress fashion of Swiss watering-places. Her pale-blue cambric dress was held up over one arm, showing her pretty feet adorned with transparent stockings and dainty, high-heeled bronze slippers.

Emily Frankland, in her beautiful home in Devonshire, was the pet and idol of all who knew her, and she had also shone as one of the brightest stars through two seasons of London gaieties; though her fresh, delicately-tinted face and bright eyes looked as if they had never been exposed to the withering effects of a ball-room.

She was of the very happy nature that adapts itself easily and contentedly to a change of scene and circumstance. So, in this quiet Swiss retreat, she forgot the monotony of her life, and lived in and enjoyed keenly the beauty of her surroundings; and on this lovely August morning she was happy as a bird, flitting about the shady paths.

With very different feelings Mr. Conway was walking along, oppressed with the burden of another day to live through, and finding fault with every mode of diversion that suggested itself.

Presently a gleam of white seen through the bushes on the lake attracted his vagrant attention, and a scream coming from the same direction quickened his languid pace. He ran to the water's side, parted the bushes, and saw Vera at some distance from the shore, leaning far out of a boat to grasp a floating oar.

"Vera, be careful!" he cried. "You will be in the water. Sit straight in the boat. Do you hear?"

"Oh, how shall I go back to the ground with no oar?"

"Where is the other oar?"

"I only took but one; the other is on the land."

"You are a very naughty little girl to go out alone on the water, and I believe I will leave you there as a punishment."

Poor Vera, already much frightened, burst into tears at hearing this threat, and buried her face in her lap. With her light golden curls falling over her bare shoulders like a veil, she looked a very pretty little picture of penitence.

Lawrence was really perplexed to know how to bring the child back to shore. The one remaining boat was turned bottom upward for repairs, and was, of course, useless. If he went away in search of help, the little girl might make more efforts to rescue herself and fall into the water. There was no one in sight or hearing, so he had resolved to adopt the unpleasant alternative of swimming out and towing her back, when a simpler expedient suggested itself. He stooped and picked up a good-sized stone, which he threw well out into the water. He saw, to his great satisfaction, that the ripple of waves made by the stone drove the little boat with its light load a trifle toward the shore. By a patient and judicious plying of stones, the little runaway might be brought safely back; so bidding Vera keep her head down and not on any account to move, he began a running fire of stones into the water, a few feet ahead of the boat.

The lake was one of the prettiest features of the hotel surroundings: graceful willows, interspersed with dark green shrubbery of all kinds, dipped and mirrored their branches around the margin of its placid bosom. The water was dazzlingly clear, and free from all the weedy growths that usually infest such tranquil lakes. Only graceful patches of water-lilies were allowed to flourish aere and there about the stony remains of a river-god who had once proudly overlooked the waters, but who had now fallen into very picturesque decay. Farther out was a pretty little island, the crowning glory of the lake. A tiny flight of marble steps, adorned on each side with a curious-shaped vase, led to a path winding through a brilliant growth of hot-house flowers, orange trees and strange foreign plants, terminating in a little rustic bower, in the window of which an æolian harp was cunningly concealed.

Nothing was more delightful than a quiet hour in this little retreat, lulled into idle dreaming by the weird soft music and the faultless beauty of the scene.

The lake was approached by a shaded path, which in its various windings gave alternate views of the water and undulating lawn, and down this path

Emily Frankland was going, idly swinging her broad-brimmed hat by its blue ribbon. Suddenly she started and grew pale. Miss Frankland, calm and collected on most occasions, as her countrywomen usually are, became perhaps too impulsive when her sympathies were aroused. She saw the crouching figure of the child in the boat, and the stones sent flying by the supposed lunatic. With a cry of terror she rushed forward and seized the bewildered Lawrence by the arm.

"If I can only get him away!" she thought, with a beating heart. "What a blessing I came when I did! In another minute he might have sunk the boat, or killed that poor child. 'Do come for a walk with me,' she said, nervously dragging at Lawrence's arm. 'I don't like the water; let us walk toward the house.' Then, seeing him hesitate, she almost screamed in her fright, 'Oh, you must come! I am afraid to go alone. Somebody is calling you. Oh, do *please* come!'"

"My dear young lady, calm yourself, I beg of you! There is nothing ——"

"Oh don't speak, but only come." And she broke into a half run, tugging the amazed Lawrence after her, who, too hopelessly bewildered to remonstrate, dropped his remaining stone and allowed himself to be forcibly borne away.

"Will you let me always here?" cried Vera, in great alarm at seeing the turn things were taking.

"No, dear; wait there very quietly; don't move till I come back; I shall not be gone long," Emily answered over her shoulder.

She hurried away across the lawn, keeping just ahead of Lawrence, and never relaxing for a moment her grasp on his arm. Suddenly an expression of relief broke over her excited face, and darting into a cross-path with a speed that nearly upset Lawrence, she hailed one of the servants, who was carrying a cup of coffee to some invisible person down the path. "François, put down the coffee and come here. Never mind, it can wait; you can go back for more."

As the man approached, Emily stopped, and putting a piece of money in his hand, said something hurriedly in a low tone which Lawrence did not understand. She then turned and looked at Lawrence for the first time since their hasty departure from the lake, and said with an imploring expression which added to our hero's confusion still more, "You will go with this man, will you not, please?"

Lawrence was devoured with curiosity concerning his fair neighbor's excitement, and a thousand questions sprang to his lips; but seeing the look on her face of painful anxiety to have him start, he restrained himself, and moved on with the man, hoping to extract some information from him, as the young lady appeared so reticent.

Emily, inexpressibly delighted at seeing him really set off, went back to the lake to wait for the servant's return to rescue Vera.

Lawrence found the servant man incomprehensible as everything else. He looked at the money in his hand with a perplexed grin, stole a furtive glance at Lawrence, looked after the retreating form of Miss Frankland, and then shook his head as though he gave the matter up. Lawrence, anxious to get at some explanation of the mystery, summoned his best French to ask the man what message the young lady had given him. The man seemed to understand the question, but failed utterly to make Lawrence comprehend his reply. He looked back to where Miss Frankland had disappeared, rubbed his forehead, pointed to the hotel, and said much which Lawrence took in all wrong, and so obtained very little enlightenment. The two plodded on together,—Lawrence anxious to tell his companion that his escort was unnecessary, but not knowing how to say it. When within a stone's throw of the hotel he turned to the man, not wishing to be escorted home in the truant school-boy fashion, and said:

"Now old fellow, slope; we are not a sociable pair, and I have had enough of your society. Go!"

Mr. Conway's meaning was plainly enough expressed by signs; so, after a moment's hesitation, the man looked toward the hotel, then back over the ground they had come, and seeming satisfied, put his money in his pocket and took his departure. Lawrence walked on to the hotel, and going up to his room took his favorite meerschaum from its case, and descending the stairs, settled himself for a smoke on a little side verandah, where he was sheltered from observation by a leafy curtain of Virginia creeper. While he is racking his brains to discover a valid reason for Miss Frankland's attack on him, we will leave him and return to the fair subject of his meditations, standing on the bank of the lake.

By the time help appeared, Mr. Conway's impromptu waves had driven the boat so near the shore that, by wading out a little, a man seized the boat and drew it to shore without difficulty.

"Thank heavens, child, you have escaped!" exclaimed Emily, lifting the little girl out of the boat.

Vera, thinking she meant from the danger of drowning, answered: "Oh *ma chère demoiselle*, I was so very afraid! But why did you tear away the nice gentleman?"

" Because he might have killed you."

" But he is very *aimable*, he do not such things."

" My dear child, you don't understand; only be glad you are not drowned."

" But was he not helping to not drown me ? "

" No, you poor little credulous thing. Are you sure he did not hurt you ? "

" Oh no, he never do that. Why think you so ? "

" Don't stop to ask questions now, little girl, but go back to the hotel with this man, and mind you do not wander any more about the place alone."

" Come you not back, too ? "

" I am going the way I came. Take care you do not get into trouble again; I might not be there a second time to help you out."

Emily flew along the winding path, and in an incredibly short space of time found herself again at her mother's side. She flung herself down, breathless, under one of the orange trees, exclaiming: " Oh mamma, such an adventure! You know that little light-haired girl we admire so much?—she was out alone in a boat. Darwin arrived just in time—I mean, I arrived—to stop him throwing stones at her. I bribed one of the waiters to take him back to the house. The poor little thing was in floods of tears; such a pile of stones he had ready to throw!

I was trembling all over with fright, when I seized his arm ——"

"My dear child, what are you talking about? Rest a moment and take breath; then, perhaps, I shall understand your exciting story."

Emily, swallowing her emotion with a convulsive gulp, went on: "I reached the lake just in time to see that crazy creature on the bank, throwing a shower of stones at the poor little girl. She had her face hidden in her lap, and looked the picture of fright. I took hold of the Count's arm and restrained him as well as I could, but at first he seemed very much inclined to resist. I succeeded in drawing him away from the lake, and was leading him across the lawn, when you can imagine my delight at seeing one of the men-servants in the distance. I called him and gave him five francs to take the Count safely back to the hotel and put him in charge of somebody. Don't you think I did quite right, mamma?"

"Yes, Emily, you were a great deal more thoughtful than I should have been in a similar case."

"But, mamma, they all acted so strangely. The man seemed struggling with a laugh, which he dared not let me see or hear. The little girl was not much frightened when I took her out of the boat, and was inclined to wonder why I had sent Count Lemanski away. As for the Count himself, his astonishment at what I did was beyond all description."

"I think, Emily, you need not feel uneasy at what these three people thought,—a child, a Swiss servant and a lunatic are all equally useless where presence of mind is necessary, as in an emergency of this kind. I think you acted very bravely."

"I tried to, at all events. I wonder that servant did not understand better what he was to do. I have seen him about the house ever since we have been here, and he must know the poor Count is an unstable character."

"The coarse .fellow probably could not restrain his amusement at the lunatic's latest freak. You are sure the little girl was in danger, Emily?"

"Why, of course, mamma. Didn't I see with my own eyes the stones flying? I do hope they will keep him shut up for a while. I shall be so frightened if I meet him again. Do you think we had better mention this to any one, mamma? Perhaps it is better not."

"I agree with you, my dear. If the little girl was very much frightened, she will, of course, complain to her mother, and it will be that lady's duty to have the danger averted, not ours. The poor young man's guardians probably know best when to confine him. The man who took him back to the house will have a long story to tell, you may be sure. I think we had much better say nothing about it. It is not a pleasant subject to discuss."

"We will let it drop, then, and when I see the Count again I will try and act as if nothing had happened; but if I have any more such encounters I certainly shall complain, for I am afraid he is more dangerous than any one supposes. Come, mamma, let us go back to the hotel, I feel tired as if I had been walking miles."

"This must have been a very disagreeable scene for you, my dear,—you are all trembling and excited yet. Lean on my arm while we walk back. You will have time to lie down a little and rest before dinner,—that will make you feel better.

"He certainly will not be at dinner,—do you think it possible, mamma?"

"Not if the man gave him in charge, as he promised you he would."

"I don't think I could sit quietly at dinner to-day opposite that black-eyed creature. He might be there. I should feel so uneasy all the time. I believe I will not go down."

"Shall we order dinner in our own rooms to-day?"

"Yes, that would be a very satisfactory arrangement. We can have it early, and go for a quiet walk afterward."

In retracing their steps to the front entrance of the hotel, the two ladies passed close along the verandah where Lawrence was still smoking, but they did not see who was behind the leafy wall. It was well for Emily's peace of mind that she did not see him, for she was at that moment ready to shriek with fright at the mere mention of the name of Count Lemanski.

Although invisible himself, Lawrence had a full view of all who passed by his retreat. "There goes that most incomprehensible of young women," he said to himself, as Emily and her mother crossed along by the verandah and disappeared. "What wouldn't I give to know what crotchet she has in her pretty head about me! What a fierce little tigress she was, as she sprang down and bore me off in her clutches! I was as weak as a kitten with sheer astonishment. And the joke of it was, she wouldn't give me a word of explanation. What did she say to that waiter fellow about me? There's not a soul I can ask about her here that would know. I must manage to find out. When Haskett comes I will try to have the mystery cleared up.

He is not such an ass about French as I am. I wonder what phase of character the English rose will show next? First, serene and cold as an iceberg,— then, in the heat of excitement, plunges down on a fellow, seizes him in an inexorable grip—how those little fingers can pinch!—and drags him away from the accomplishment of a good work! By Jove! what has become of Vera all this time?"

Mr. Conway started up, left his pipe on the seat behind him, and went in search of his little Russian friend.

CHAPTER V.

HIS PERPLEXITIES INCREASE.

EMILY had so far recovered from the fright of her adventure at the lake as to be able to laugh at the recollection of it on the following morning. She had not seen the Count since giving him in charge of the servant, and she believed he was in safe custody for the present. She took a book with her this morning and walked toward the shade of a wide-spreading lime tree for a quiet half hour alone. Within a short distance of the tree she opened her book, and went slowly along, reading, till, with a start and half scream, she almost stumbled over Lawrence Conway, who was stretched at full length on the turf at the other side of the tree. He had broken off a branch from the lime tree, and was idly twisting it about, to the frantic delight of a small kitten which had strayed toward him.

Emily's first thought was to beat a precipitate retreat, but a second glance showed her that the young gentleman was quite calm and docile looking. She felt emboldened and reassured, and went a step nearer. On seeing her, Lawrence gathered himself up hastily and made an effort to take off his hat, but as that article was lying on the grass beside him, the motion was attended with no result.

Emily was at a loss, at first, to know how to address him, but remembering what Winnie had told her about the happy results of conversing with him on his favorite subject, said, with a sweet smile, hoping to ward off any unpleasant demonstration on his part: "It cannot be a very dreadful punishment for a soul to be imprisoned in such a pretty, graceful body."

At Lawrence's look of utter bewilderment Emily felt much alarm.

"To whose body are you referring?—if I may ask," he said, eyeing his own comely proportions.

"Why, the kitten's, of course! You know the bodies of all animals are only the prisons of human souls," Emily ventured, fearing he was not going to prove tractable, and wishing she had not spoken to him at all.

"Why, the girl's cracked—moon-struck—mad as a March hare!" thought Lawrence. "I'll try humoring her queer ideas. Can she be only joking?"

"Quite true," he answered, aloud. "It is very

curious to think that the most insignificant puppy
one meets may turn out to be one's best friend."

"We must be so careful in our conduct and re-
marks in the presence of animals. A great many
important secrets must have been spread abroad by
people discussing them carelessly—in the presence of
dogs and horses, for instance."

"I don't doubt it," Lawrence answered, emphatically.

"Do you not find it very much against your conscience to eat meat and fowl? It is almost cannibal-
ism."

"I have no scruples against it," Lawrence replied
gravely; "for when the animal or chicken is killed,
the soul is liberated."

"He reasons as if he had thought a great deal on
this absurd subject; and how perfectly he speaks
English," Emily said to herself. "Do you still read
aloud to the spirit of the donkey?" she continued,
aloud, with a great show of interest.

"Yes, and I find him very attentive. He listens
for hours, and never interrupts with a single question. There is wonderful concentrative power in a
donkey."

"I wonder if this is the beginning of the flow of
eloquence Winnie talked about?" Emily asked herself.

The attention of the deluded pair was momentarily distracted by the appearance on the scene of a bare-footed, saucy-eyed boy. He was driving a flock of geese across the lawn, giving lively thumps with a hooked stick to those of his charge who were inclined to loiter.

"Oh, my unhappy sisters!" exclaimed Emily, clasping her hands and rolling her brown eyes sentimentally from the geese to Lawrence.

"What a sympathetic soul you have," he answered, mentally agreeing with her as to the relationship.

How exactly Winnie understood his case! "The poor fellow's brain is completely turned!"

"Do you have such fine scenery as this in Poland?" Emily resumed presently, trying what effect a change of subject would have.

"I do not know, I never was there."

"Indeed! I had understood you were a Pole."

"No, I am an American."

"He is not even clear about his own identity," Emily mused, saying aloud: "I am English. We are almost of the same country."

"So near, and yet so far," observed Lawrence.

"What phase of existence do you expect to arrive at next?" pursued Emily.

"I want to be an angel," he answered, making

heroic efforts to keep his face straight, but succeeding badly.

"Does he think of killing himself?" Emily asked herself uneasily. "What strange faces he makes!"

"Do you find the time pass pleasantly here?" she asked; "or had you rather be elsewhere?"

"I find it abominably dull, except when some benignant angel, like yourself, smiles on me and brightens the dark hours."

"Oh dear, is he going to be friendly? What will mamma say?"

"Have you many acquaintances here?"

"No, very few; but I am expecting a friend soon,—a fellow I went on some excursions with last year; and when he comes I shall have something to do in looking at all the show-places about here."

"How nice that will be for you! Is your friend in human guise?" Emily asked, with a sweetly innocent expression on her pretty face.

"When I saw him last he was an unmistakable specimen of the *genus homo*. He may possibly have changed since."

"You would be disappointed if he came in the form of a lap-dog, would you not?"

"I confess it would interfere with my plans. But I hardly think he would make over well into a dog."

"What form would he be most likely to take?"

"He has been frequently called a brick, and likened to a queer fish, and an old fox. He might appear in any of these forms."

"Is he Polish also?"

"No, he is an Englishman, about my own age."

"Was he ever a Pole?"

"As far as I know, he never was."

"Do you think he ever will be?"

"Not unless you pronounce him a stick."

Emily glanced up quickly to see if he was making fun of her; but as he had resolved not to be astonished at anything this young lady might say or do, his face was imperturbable.

"Tell me more about your friend. Is he nice? What does he look like?" asked Emily, forgetting that the description could hardly be accurate.

"He is a very fair sort of fellow,—rather too much of a dandy. He has blue eyes, curly hair and red cheeks. Do you like that kind of man?"

"I prefer dark men; but appearances go for very little. Does he dance well?"

"The girls say he waltzes like—oh, like an angel. I believe that is a proper comparison."

"What a delightful acquisition he will be! When is he coming?"

"Probably in a few days."

"Is he going to stay long?"

"That I cannot tell you. I believe he does not know himself."

Lawrence here began to think his friend had been sufficiently discussed; so, to change the subject, he said:

"You seem to enjoy yourself here, Miss Frankland. What is the secret of it?"

"Oh, you know my name! Then I shall not have to introduce myself."

"My curiosity was excited when you came, and I consulted the strangers list,— to very good effect, you see."

"As to whether I like it here,— yes, I do. I find the time goes very pleasantly. It is very quiet, of course; but mamma and I are both fond of walking. I read and practice a little, when I can have a piano in comparative solitude. Then I go to the music every day, and watch what the other people do."

"Do you find the other people interesting?"

"I know very few yet. Are you trying the Saline cure, Count Lemanski?"

"Yes. I have something the matter with my head."

Lawrence wondered how he came by the name of

Lemanski,—with a title, too; but thought it all of a piece with the other vagaries of the young lady.

" The poor fellow! He knows how he is afflicted." And she gave Lawrence a look of heart-felt sympathy, which he utterly failed to understand. " But how sensibly he talks just now! I had almost forgotten he was mad."

"Are you going to the concert this evening, Miss Frankland? The programme is unusually good."

" Of course we shall go. There is never anything else to do in the evenings."

" Would you take pity on a poor waif, like myself, and permit him to join you there for a delightful half hour? You have no idea how lonely I am here."

" I suppose the poor creature feels neglected," Emily said to herself, and with her tender heart overflowing with pity, she said eagerly:

" Do come with us whenever you think it would amuse you. I take a very deep interest in you, and should so like to be your friend, and do all I could to make you happy and contented."

" You are really too kind!" exclaimed Lawrence, much struck by this burst of candor. " I should be most happy to avail myself of your friendly proposals."

" I am sure you would be better if you were more with other people —— "

Emily stopped suddenly, blushing crimson.

"Oh, what have I said? I could not have been more foolish! I have deliberately begged him to follow us about, when I knew the consequences might be something dreadful. Oh, how shall I get rid of him, and what shall I do? He spoke so feelingly, and seemed so intelligent and gentle, I quite forgot myself. Oh, Winnie, I wish you had not told me about this horrid creature, and left him to my tender mercies. What shall I do?"

Emily, in her confusion, did not know what to say next, and heartily wished to put an end to the interview. She was in doubt whether to mention the concert again or trust to the hope that the lunatic would forget about it. Her uneasy cogitations were interrupted by the approach of a man bearing a letter upon a salver. The man bowed respectfully and said:

"Do I address Mademoiselle Frankland?"

"Yes."

"Madame Frankland desired me to bring this letter to mademoiselle."

Emily took the letter, and to her great delight recognized the chirography of her devoted friend, Winnie.

Lawrence concluded that his presence might now be dispensed with, and with a remark to the effect that he would leave her to read her letter in peace, he went away in the direction of the hotel.

"How very considerate of him," thought Emily. "The more I see of him the more I am inclined to forget his infirmity. Now, what does this child say?" She broke open the letter, which was short, and ran as follows:

MY DEAR EMILY,—I have five minutes' time to write and tell you that that abominable Miss Exham is going to be married in Dresden on the 25th. She is a great friend of ours, you know, and we have got to go to the wedding. This will delay our return to Bex several weeks, as mamma wants to see Berlin while we are in that locality. I'm utterly disgusted with the whole arrangement. Will write particulars when in a better temper. Savagely yours,

WINNIE.

P. S.— How do you find Darwin?

For the first time since her arrival at the *Hôtel des Salines* Emily felt low-spirited and unhappy. It was a keen disappointment to her to think that probably her entire stay in that locality would be spent without the society of her friend, and she went slowly back to the hotel with very gloomy thoughts, in which Darwin and his unpleasantly social disposition had no share.

The band was putting itself in proper order for the afternoon, or evening concert, as it was called, and there was the usual amount of preliminary thumping and squeaking peculiar to such occasions.

All that afternoon Emily had declared her intention of not going to the music, but seeing her mother was unusually anxious to attend, she changed her mind. As the tuning of the instruments caught her ear she started up, and said it was time to go.

"It is much earlier than we usually go, Emily dear. We shall find no one there," Mrs. Frankland remonstrated mildly.

"So much the better, mamma; we do not want to elbow our way through a crowd of people."

It was entirely unlike Emily to want to escape the cheerful assemblage that met to hear the music, and Mrs. Frankland was puzzled; but she said nothing, and taking her lacework in its much-bedecked basket, followed her daughter out in the direction of the concert-ground. Furthermore, Emily displayed an unaccountable desire to avoid the seats and promenades most frequented by the fashionable part of the audience, and chose instead a bench at some distance from the others, almost invisible behind a laurel bush. Mrs. Frankland was not in favor of such strict retirement, but she concluded it best not to demur, as her daughter's temper, ever since the receipt of Winnie's letter, had been much ruffled. Half an hour passed rather slowly, as neither of the ladies were inclined to talk; after which the empty chairs and walks became alive with people, and the musicians were doing their best.

Emily was absorbed in watching the movements of Lawrence Conway, who had appeared on the scene, and was wandering about the various groups, apparently in search of some one.

"He will never find me here, thanks to the laurel-bush," said Emily in an undertone.

Lawrence walked from end to end of the concert-ground several times, and at last attracted the attention of his little friend Vera. She broke loose from a group of other children with whom she was skipping rope, and ran after him.

"Do you look for the pretty lady you like to speak with?" she asked. "For I did see her with Madame her mother go to sit on that great bush, over, *par là*, do you see?" And the little figure flew back to her companions.

Lawrence, smiling at the child's quickness of perception, turned toward the spot indicated.

"He is coming this way—he has seen us! He has all the cunning of a madman, or he would never have found us out here."

But Emily, in spite of herself, could not help feeling a kind of guilty pleasure at his approach. It was so dull sitting there away from the other people, and an agreeable, handsome cavalier, even if he was a little cracked, was far better than none. Emily found the half dozen *harmless* young gentlemen stopping at the hotel very uninteresting.

Lawrence approached the ladies, and taking his hat off expressed his pleasure at finding them after his long search. He entered into a sprightly conversation, which charmed even Mrs. Frankland, and she forgot herself so far as to laugh and chat at some length in return. Presently a lady, with whom Mrs. Frankland had struck up an acquaintance, joined the group. Emily rose and offered her her place on the seat beside her mother; this afforded Lawrence an excellent opportunity to ask Miss Frankland to stroll about with him a little among the other people. Emily expressed herself willing, and receiving a look from her mother expressive of mingled consent, disapproval and caution, walked slowly away with her fine-looking attendant. Many were the glances and whispered exclamations of admiration as the well-matched couple wandered up and down the wide lawn.

"That is a fine selection from ' *Don Juan* ' they are playing now, is it not, Miss Frankland?"

"It is beautiful — the only part of the opera that I care much for. Are you very fond of music, Count?"

"I could worship it like a god. What would I not give to be a fine musician!"

"Perhaps you will wake up some day and find yourself a great musical genius."

"That would be a delightful transformation,— even under the form of a nightingale, it would not be a bad idea."

"Are you not sometimes haunted with the fear of being changed into something disagreeable, or horrible,— like a toad or a spider," continued Emily, "and perhaps never being changed back?"

"Some people cannot arrive at a worse state than their natural one."

"Oh, I don't agree with you! Now, for instance, when you were an owl, you must have felt a deep sense of humiliation. Was it not so?"

"I do not remember my sensations in the least, while in the form of that melancholy bird. In fact, if I could do so without contradicting you, I should declare I never was an owl," Lawrence remarked, emphatically.

A finely executed violin solo silenced the young people for five minutes,— then Emily resumed:

"I heard from Miss Evans this morning,—she desired to be remembered to you."

"Very kind of her, I am sure. Pray give her my compliments. I would perhaps send something more, if I had the pleasure of knowing who she was."

"You have forgotten her, I see; she is a great friend of mine."

"I should like to know Miss Evans; she must be a lady of very good taste."

Emily was silent for a while. "I wonder if he will have forgotten all about me by next week,— or to-morrow, perhaps? I hope not."

"What do you think I am most like, Count Lemanski?" she asked, when her dreaming was over.

"You are the most delightful enigma in the world, —one I could study forever"—was on the tip of his tongue, but Lawrence restrained himself, and made some commonplace remark about requiring time to answer the question.

Too much absorbed in each other to notice where their idle footsteps were leading them, Lawrence and his fair-haired companion had wandered far away from the other people. Gradually their conversation had taken a different turn,—equally foolish, perhaps, as the foregoing, but more interesting

to the persons concerned,— being that sort of dia-
logue in which young people of opposite sexes, who
admire each other, are prone to indulge; which,
while meaning nothing, verges close on the borders
of love-making.

"Why do you call me 'Count,' Miss Frankland?
I have no title, and my name is not Lemanski.
I should have told you before, my name is——"

"But I would much rather call you Count Lemanski,— let it rest so, will you not?"

It jarred on Emily to have her companion so
soon relapse into his wandering strain, and she felt
in no mood to listen to whatever fantastic name
he might give himself.

"So be it," answered Lawrence. "What's in a
name?"

These few words had the effect of awaking both
from their pleasant dream. Lawrence saw that the
young girl's thoughts had drifted back into their
crooked channel, and Emily remembered, with alarm,
that after all her companion was a madman, and
they were far from home. "What if he would not
let me turn back?"

But nothing so unpleasant happened, and when
she proposed returning, Lawrence, without a demur,
escorted her back to where Mrs. Frankland was

sitting. That lady received her daughter with an air of relief that seemed to say, "I never expected to see you alive again, my child." Lawrence walked back to the house with the ladies, and when he had left them, Emily exclaimed:

"Oh, mamma! what is it about that man that is so mysterious? The more I see of him, the more I am puzzled. He was really quite charming to-day,—he talked nonsense as well as any of the gentlemen one meets in London, and was so collected and natural. Why can't he always be so?"

"My dear child, I am afraid you are letting your sympathies get the better of you. I don't deny that there is something very prepossessing about this poor young gentleman,—and for that reason he is all the more dangerous, as in talking to him one is made to forget his weak points. I wish you would not wander off out of sight with him again, as you did to-day. It is not safe, and it will excite remark among the other people. Remember, you have seen him at a disadvantage,—the day he was throwing stones at the little Russian girl, for instance, and the slightest provocation may make him frighten you again. Will you promise me to be more discreet, Emily?"

Emily had been paying very little attention to

her mother's warning words, and her mind was far away as she answered; but Mrs. Frankland seemed satisfied, and began to talk of other things.

Lawrence Conway, on his balcony that night, lazily enjoying the moonlight, saw in the wreaths of smoke that curled up from his cigar, the shadowy form of a beautiful, fair-haired girl, her brown eyes shining on him with a half-frightened, half trustful gaze, and her fair arms extended tenderly toward him, or drawn timidly away with an unaccountable caprice. Far into the night he sat there, till the moon, tired of trying to win his errant attention, drew a cloudy veil over her face and stole out of sight. Then he rose, saying over and over to himself, "Why is she not always as she was tonight?" But he was not referring to the moon.

CHAPTER VI.

IN WHICH PRUDENCE WAS NOT A VIRTUE.

BEFORE Lawrence had left his room the next day, a card was handed to him, with the name "Mr. Sidney Haskett," inscribed thereon. "Why, the old fellow's ahead of time,—so much the better for me. Show him up, man,—and be quick about it"—he said to the servant awaiting his orders. In a moment more, a gentleman with a handsome, rather cynical face, entered the room. He had bright blue eyes, a straight, clear-cut nose, crisp, curling, light hair, and a complexion that many a woman might have envied. His figure, though graceful and well proportioned, fell an inch or two below the ordinary height of men, and this was the only point in which Sidney Haskett admitted that he failed. The good opinion he had of himself led him to regard the rest of mankind,—and womankind, too,—in a very unfavorable light; and it was owing to his exalted ideal of what the future wife of his bosom should be, that his twenty-ninth birthday found him still enjoying a state of single blessedness.

84

When there was no one present to admire him —(he was an only son, and heir to a fine estate and fortune)—he forgot himself, in a measure, and was much more agreeable. It was during a few days spent in Vienna, mostly sight-seeing, and 'roughing it' for a month in the Tyrol, that Lawrence had known and liked him. He had yet to discover what he was in polite society. The long chat between the two gentlemen, about mutual friends and past events, has nothing to do with our story, until Lawrence gradually merged into a description of their probable undertakings and present surroundings.

"There is a young lady here," he went on, "who is a wonderful study. She is very pretty,— soft, brown eyes, with blonde hair, a lovely complexion, and the sweetest voice and manners in the world."

"Why, Conway, it is a clear case of the *grande passion* with you already!"

"No it isn't. Could you fall in love with a girl who is half-witted?"

"Certainly not. Is your charmer more lacking in brains than most women? If that were the case, I couldn't get up an interest in her, even if she had the beauty of a Venus and Juno combined."

"Wait a little, till you see her. One instant this

young lady of waom I speak is everything that is
charming; the next, she will wander off into a wonderful discussion about the souls of puppies and
kittens, and tell you long stories about astonishing
cases of transformation, asking your opinion in the
gravest way. On the subject of transmigration of
souls, she is undoubtedly cracked; but she is a con-
sistent little lunatic, and never rambles on any other
topic; and she talks about other things as well as
anybody. You must see her, and talk to her. I
want to have some one else's opinion about her.
Sometimes I think I have been deluding myself all
along, and that she is just as sane as I am. But
she does say and do most unaccountable things."

"Oh, I see. You are prepared to fall in love with
her, but cannot reconcile it with your conscience
under existing circumstances. I am to declare the
young lady sane, and in her right mind, and thereby
do away with your scruples."

For some reason Lawrence could not help thinking
that Haskett did not seem as nice a fellow as he was
before.

After a comfortable dinner in a cosy little private
room, Lawrence escorted his friend out to see the
grounds. Their way led past the croquet-ground,
where a game was going on between Miss Frankland

and her thin admirer, Vera and a white-haired English Admiral. Mrs. Frankland was seated at a convenient distance, overlooking the game with bland interest.

"There she is, Haskett!" said Lawrence, with a slight pressure of his companion's arm. "The pretty girl in white."

"Both young ladies answer to your description,— blonde-haired, pretty, and with white dresses," Mr. Haskett answered, with a laugh. "But I will give you the credit of having chosen the grown-up one. She is rather pretty."

"You are altogether too clever, Haskett. But the little girl is not far behind the other, except in years."

A moment after, Vera, with a triumphant shout, waving her mallet, rushed up and hugged the knees of her silver-haired partner, crying: "Oh, my darling, the play is to we! *Mon Dieu, que je suis contente!*"

This caused a general laugh, after which the party broke up, and Lawrence took the opportunity to introduce his friend to Mrs. Frankland and her daughter.

As they were all walking back to the hotel together, Mrs. Frankland was charmed at the discovery that the new-comer knew, intimately, dear friends of hers

in England. Whereupon she grew quite confidential,
and recalled a visit she had made once, in days gone
by, at the house of Sidney Haskett's father. The
memory of that time made her heart overflow with
cordiality toward the young man, and he felt himself,
figuratively, taken to her bosom. It was a great piece
of good luck, too, she thought, that such a prepossessing gentleman should arrive just in time to divert
Emily's thoughts from dwelling too much on that
unfortunate young Pole. A few hours later Emily
was walking by the lake, where by some strange
chance Mr. Conway met her.

"May I row you over to the island, Miss Frankland?"

"Oh yes! I was wanting so much to go out on the
water, but was too lazy to row myself."

"How glad I am that I can be of some use to you!
Have you a choice of boats? They are both in order
now, I believe," Lawrence said, bending over one of
the oars.

In the meantime Emily remembered the last time
she had seen him at the lake, and felt frightened. It
would be too much risk to trust herself on that
broad, deep lake with this man alone. He was a
maniac after all, and, much as the refusal cost her,
she dared not venture. All this time Lawrence was

holding the boat,—the "Péri," it was called,—so she should not wet her little slippers in stepping in.

"I believe I won't go," she said hesitatingly.

"Not go! Are you afraid, Miss Emily?"

"No," she said with a blush; "but I have changed my mind. I don't want to go. I might be—sea-sick!" she answered, with another vivid blush at the enormity of this suggestion, on that motionless sheet of water.

"But you said that you would like to go, and I thought——" But seeing she was nervously digging at the pebbles with her parasol, and biting her lips, not knowing how to answer him, Lawrence left his remark unfinished, and with a light laugh at this abrupt refusal, but feeling hurt and disappointed all the same, he got into the boat alone.

"If you should change your mind, I hope you will call me back, Miss Frankland," he said, as he pushed slowly off in the direction of the island. Emily did change her mind, as soon as the boat left the shore, and she felt much inclined to quarrel with herself as Lawrence glided away, trifling with his oars, as if to be in readiness to return for her if she should still care to come. Should she call him back and go over to the enchanted island? A faint echo from the harp in the window struck her ear. It was very tempting.

But no; pride and prudence mastered her, and she did not recall the graceful oarsman, who was furtively watching her from under his eyelids; till at last, as she turned and resumed her walk on the shore, he bent to his oars and sent the little skiff flying over the smooth water, and was soon out of sight behind a curve in the shore.

Emily was startled from her unpleasant reverie by a voice saying, almost in her ear: "Do you prefer being alone, Miss Frankland, or may I intrude on your solitude? I hope I have not frightened you?"

"No, it is nothing; but I didn't hear a sound till you spoke. You must have a very light footstep. You do not intrude, Mr. Haskett. I was feeling very tired, bored, and cross with myself, and I am glad you have come to talk me into a better temper."

"Thank you; you will make me quite proud of myself if you let me think I have the power to chase away your feeling of *ennui*," Mr. Haskett replied, accommodating his pace to hers.

"Why are you not out on the water, Miss Frankland?"

"I did not care to row myself."

"An English girl, and not fond of boating!—that is very unusual."

"But I do like it, and I want to go. Will you take me?"

Emily had an uncontrollable desire to go over to the island. She glanced uneasily in the direction where Lawrence had disappeared, but no signs of him were to be seen. Then she quieted her conscience with the thought that she had asked Mr. Haskett to row her, and therefore she was not accepting from him an invitation that she had refused from her afflicted friend. After all, it was foolish, perhaps, to trouble herself about it, for the Count would not perceive a slight, as other men would. So, when Mr. Haskett declared himself her devoted slave, to row to the island, or anywhere she pleased, she conquered her hesitation, and stepped into the remaining boat.

"I'm sorry I have not a larger space to give you a proof of my rowing powers, Miss Frankland. I was considered a very good stroke at Oxford."

"There is plenty of room to astonish such an unsophisticated person as myself. It is a pity there are no dangers connected with our voyage that I could admire your skill in escaping."

"You are not a timid young lady, then?"

"Oh yes!—dreadfully so."

"I must find out in what way, so I can avoid frightening you."

Mr. Conway, in the meantime, had been exhausting his superfluous energies in a vigorous pull around the lake. Tired with this exercise, he paddled slowly toward one of the clumps of water-lilies doing their best to conceal the wreck of the river-god. He leaned over and gathered a quantity of the finest blossoms and half-opened buds, and piled them up in the bow of his boat. This occupation finished, he sprinkled the flowers thoroughly to keep them fresh, and pulling under the shade of a willow not far from the shore, shipped his oars and tried to stretch himself for a snooze; but finding a reclining position uncomfortable under the circumstances, he sat up again, and took a note-book from his pocket, the contents of which he began to scan with a fair show of interest. His attention was attracted from this by the even plashing of another pair of oars.

"So that is your game, my fickle young lady!" he exclaimed to himself, as he saw the boat containing Emily and Mr. Haskett skimming along toward the island.

"You can refuse point-blank to go out in the boat with me, and then under my very eyes accept the invitation of the next man that comes along. I knew what you said about sea-sickness was all humbug. What an insinuating way that fellow Haskett has about him! She seems quite taken with him already," he muttered between his teeth as he saw Mr. Haskett rest on his oars and bend toward his fair companion with an air of admiring attention to what she was saying. Then he answered something which made her turn away with a slight blush and a half smile, and begin to dabble her pretty white hand in the water. "Confound his impudence!" Lawrence thought, and he gave a rueful glance at the water-lilies piled up in the stern of his boat. Is it beneath a man's dignity to quarrel with a half-witted girl? I wish she were not so seductively pretty and interesting. She never smiled as much on me in a week as she has on this fellow in half an hour. She is a capricious little flirt, after all. What an infernal muddle these accounts are in!" he exclaimed, as he turned again to the note-book.

While Lawrence was meditating thus, Emily and Mr. Haskett had reached the island and disembarked. They ascended the marble steps, and went on through the deliciously fragrant path.

"Oh, don't you know it's 'defended' to pick the flowers!" Emily cried gaily, as her companion pulled down a branch of an orange tree and took a handful of the sweet blossoms.

"I hardly think they will call *me* to account for it," he answered, confidently. They reached the little flower-grown arbor, and Emily sat on the step barring the entrance.

"No admittance," she said, looking at him with a provoking smile.

"Not if I pay toll?" he asked, arranging the orange blossoms in a graceful cluster, and offering them to her.

"Thank you," she said, fastening them in the bosom of her dress. He then took another spray and dropped it lightly and deftly among the heap of soft curls on her bowed head; it lodged there as if by magic, and the effect was charming.

"Orange blossoms are not an appropriate decoration for you, but they are vastly becoming."

"Sit down on that stump, Mr. Haskett. I want to talk to you seriously about your friend. Is there any chance of his poor head being set right again? He seems so well now I should think his friends would have great hopes."

Mr. Haskett, stretching himself on the soft grass beside the stump indicated, was astonished to hear so much solicitude on the part of a stranger for an ailment on which Lawrence himself had never bestowed an anxious thought.

"I believe he is rather better," he said, "but as his symptoms never get any worse, they are not alarming."

"But isn't it bad enough as it is? Just think what his poor mother must suffer! Do you know her?"

"I saw her once in Vienna. A very handsome woman, and very agreeable, too. She said a good deal about her son's weakness, and hoped the air and water of this place was going to do wonders for him."

"Is it not a great trial to her to have such a son? and he an only child, too."

"I believe she does groan over his shortcomings occasionally,— or ought to, at least."

"Such a handsome young man as he is, and so intelligent at times! Think what he might be if he had full possession of his reason! If I had not heard it from the best authority, I could hardly believe he was insane."

This enigmatical conversation was beginning to clear itself before the mental vision of Sidney Haskett.

"But he has many lucid moments, and is never dangerous, so his is not a bad case of its kind," Mr. Haskett answered, concealing the smile that would distort the corners of his mouth, by picking at the ivy covering the stump against which he leaned.

"But all the same it is very sad. The poor young

man interests me more than I can express. He is so much more like an Englishman than a Pole. I suppose that adds to my interest."

"Your tender heart does you credit, Miss Frankland. I am sure my poor friend would be immensely flattered if he could know of and appreciate your friendly feeling for him. But suppose we talk of something else; his affliction is a dreary subject?"

"Perhaps I have been indiscreet in mentioning the subject, Mr. Haskett; you may not like to hear the failing of your friend discussed by a stranger?"

"Pray do not say that, Miss Frankland; no one could mistake your kindly sympathy for annoying curiosity. I can hardly regard you as a stranger; perhaps I ought to, but it seems as if I had known - you for a very long time, and it was only yesterday we met."

Mr. Haskett, for private reasons, wished to keep the conversation away from his friend Conway, and by a few judicious questions succeeded in launching Emily into a long description of her stay at the *Hôtel des Salines,* her life in England, her friend Winnie, and many similar topics.

Mr. Haskett lounged idly back and watched her through his half-closed eyes, more intent on admiring her pretty face and graceful figure and motions than in listening to what she said. This bright-eyed, sunny-haired girl was no half-witted phenomenon such as Conway had represented. On the contrary, she was unusually clever and intelligent. There was some grand mistake somewhere. How it arose he could not for the moment discover, nor did he care to. It was so pleasant lying there on the cool grass, watching his pretty companion talking to him so charmingly. She seemed satisfied with his few lazy answers. If the subject of Conway came up again he would have to exert himself to do most of the talking. He would clear up the misunderstanding later, when his head felt clearer. His thoughts were all wandering now.

A little breeze had sprung up, and suddenly a faint moaning cry, half human, half ghostly, was heard.

"What was that!" exclaimed Mr. Haskett, starting up.

"Be quiet a moment," said Emily, softly laying her hand for an instant on his arm.

Then it came again, very sweet and clear at first, then sobbing itself away in a faint echo. Again the musical sound arose and fell, changed into a joyful tinkling, and died suddenly.

"Did you never hear an æolian harp, Mr. Haskett?"

"Never but once. There are some in the old castle at Baden-Baden. I had forgotten the sound."

"It is a melancholy thing, is it not?" Emily said, as another sweep of the magic fingers was heard.

"Come, let us go back. It makes me think all kinds of gloomy things to-day. I will row back, Mr. Haskett; you seem tired,— or perhaps it is only laziness."

"It is neither one nor the other — only regret at leaving this very delightful little spot."

"We will come here again, when there is not a breath of wind."

"I shall watch the weather closely after this, Miss Frankland."

They wound their way slowly back, through the luxuriant path, down the steps and into the little boat.

"Shall we return directly to land, Miss Frankland, or would you like to go around the lake? I can send this little boat flying, with her light load."

"Yes, let us have an imaginary race. I want something to stir me up and make me forget that harp."

They skimmed along with a speed that would have been alarming on any other water. Lawrence watched them from under his shady cover, aroused by Emily's merry laugh. They came nearer to where he was.

He hoped they would not discover him in his shady
retreat, for he felt too hurt and angry to chime in
with their gay mood.   His hopes were realized and
his little nook was not discovered, for within twenty
yards of where he lay, the swiftly flying boat struck·
against a fragment of the ruined water-god, shot up
and capsized.   There was a scream and two persons
struggling in the water.   Mr. Haskett came to the
surface instantly, but he seemed dazed and unable to
collect his scattered senses.   He clung forlornly to the
overturned boat, shivering and helpless, and drabbled
with mud and weeds.   It was his own palpable carelessness that caused the accident, and perhaps this
thought overwhelmed him.   It was most fortunate for
Emily that a man who could retain his presence of
mind in an emergency was ready for her rescue.
Quick as thought, Lawrence tore off his coat, sprang
into the water, seized her around the waist and lifted
her into his boat before she had time to lose consciousness.   After much shivering and convulsive effort to
regain her breath, she ejaculated:

"Oh, Count Lemanski, how can I ever thank you
enough!   You are soaking wet.   We are all drowned,
what shall we do?"

"Get dry things as soon as possible.   But, my dear
Miss Frankland, don't, I beg of you, waste your

strength in thanks. You will need it all when the reaction after your fright comes. You are wonderfully brave."

"Come, Haskett, old fellow, have you got a chill? Your teeth are chattering like a pair of castanets."

Lawrence gave him a hand into his boat and the dripping trio were pulled rapidly back to shore. There was a lady in a wheeled chair making frantic gestures to them from the bank, who suggested all kinds of impossible remedies when they landed. But her presence was most opportune in one way, for when Emily tried to step, her wet garments clung to her so tightly that walking was almost impossible. Whereupon the invalid lady insisted on Emily taking her chair to be wheeled back to the house, as she could sit on a bench in the meantime. This kindly suggestion was acted on, and Emily, enveloped in shawls and wraps, was borne away by the lady's attendant, and the two gentlemen started off at full speed across the lawn in search of dry garments. Lawrence came back an hour afterward, none the worse for his dip, to review the scene of the accident. The disabled boat had been towed to shore, and seeing there was nothing to be done he was turning away, when the heap of water-lilies in the bow of the "Péri" caught his eye. They were still fresh and beautiful as when gathered. He called a gardener at work in the neighborhood, and, pointing to the lilies, gave him some instructions in German, together with a blank card which he took from his pocket, on which he wrote a few words in pencil.

CHAPTER VII.

A FALSE FRIEND.

BEYOND a slight headache, Miss Frankland felt no unpleasant results from her dip in the lake, and it was only to gratify her mother, who begged her to go to bed till even this slight indisposition should wear off, that she did not appear in public again that evening.

She was sitting up in bed, in the prettiest of lace-adorned night-gowns. Vera was sprawled across the foot of the bed, drumming with her small, white-shod feet against the foot-board, and singing stray little bits of songs, or listening with deep attention to Emily's account of her ducking. In the middle of her story there came a knock at the door, which Vera flew to answer.

"Oh, Miss Emily!—look, look at the beautiful flowers! Bring them in, Maurice."

The servant carried in and set in the window a gracefully-shaped basket, brimming over with a profusion of water-lilies, exquisitely arranged with a variety of moss and trailing ferns. There was a card tied to the handle, which Vera eagerly tore off and brought to Emily, who read the words: "To Undine, with the compliments of Count Lemanski."

"Are they not of my friend who drew you out of the water?— he is so *gentil*," Vera said.

"Yes, dear. They are very pretty. What a nice idea of the poor fellow!"

"Oh, he is so much nice!—better than the small gentleman with so many sharp tooth. May I make your hair, Miss Emily, with some lilies in it? I will not derange the basket."

"Yes, little one, if it would amuse you; but I am not going to get up this evening, so it will be labor lost, unless I go to sleep in them."

"Oh, that makes nothing. I go to make you so beautiful!" With deft fingers the little girl selected some of the smallest blossoms and trailing buds, and wound them in Emily's pretty hair, showing an innate taste and artistic love of beauty very rare in a child of her years.

"Oh, but you are an angel now! Look!" she cried, in an ecstasy of delight at her own handiwork, pushing a swinging glass to where Emily could see the reflection of her pretty self.

"What a little coquette you will be some day, Vera,

if you turn your taste for decorating other people toward your own little self."

"Will I be like you, Miss Emily, when I grow to be a great lady?"

"I can't tell, Vera; would you like to be?"

"Oh, so much! But I will tell the nice black-eye gentleman to come and see how I have made arrange his flowers. It will please him many." She was darting out of the room, when Emily caught her by her short petticoats.

"No, Vera, child, you must not call him. English ladies don't receive visits from gentlemen when they are in bed. The gentleman would be very much astonished if you asked him to come to see me."

"Will you, then, wear more flower in your hairs when you go downstairs to-morrow?"

"Perhaps I will. Vera, I'm tired, will you sing me to sleep?" Emily lay back and closed her eyes, while the child slipped to the floor, clasped her little hands in front of her, and standing at Emily's pillow, sang in a sweet childish voice the plaintive little Russian cradle-song beginning "Sleep, thou infant angel, sleep." She then stole softly out of the room, shutting the door noiselessly after her. Emily opened her eyes with a smile when she had disappeared. "Dear little girl! She is more companionable than half the grown-up people one meets. But I must not go to sleep with poor Darwin's flowers in my hair. How good of him to rush to my rescue as he did! The poor fellow seems to be trying to make me forget all his eccentricities by his quiet, thoughtful behavior now. His friend is very agreeable and interesting. I can't decide whether I like him or not; he has a way of looking at one which is sometimes annoying. On the whole, I think I do like him. What with Darwin turning out a hero and Mr. Haskett presenting himself for a flirtation, this quiet place is becoming quite exciting."

When Mrs. Frankland came in to see if her daughter was comfortably settled for the night, she went into raptures over the basket of lilies, till Emily told her who had sent them.

"Count Lemanski!" she said, as her face fell. "I thought, of course, they were from Mr. Haskett."

"Mr. Haskett is not so devoted as my crazy friend, you see, mamma."

"I wish you would not talk in that light way, -Emily; Count Lemanski has you already a great deal too much in his thoughts. But you are tired this evening, I will not give you a scolding."

"One would have to be very tired and weak, mamma dear, not to be able to bear one of your scoldings," said Emily, patting her mother's cheek; "but what were you going to say?"

"I was going to suggest that now Mr. Haskett is here, whom I know to be a gentleman in every respect, you need not depend in the very least on this unfortunate Pole for society."

"Oh, mamma dear, you need not be alarmed. I am not going to do anything more dreadful than to wear some of Darwin's lilies in my hair to-morrow, to let him know, in the simplest way, that they have been received."

"Emily, you could not do anything that would annoy me more. I beg of you not to do anything so foolish. It would keep up his interest, and you want him to forget you as soon as possible,—I mean Count Lemanski, not Mr. Haskett. Will you remember what I say, Emily?"

"We will not talk about it any more to-night, dear. I do feel tired, and want to go to sleep."

Mrs. Frankland left the room, and Emily fell into a confused dream of Mr. Haskett, raving mad, struggling to drown Darwin, with Winnie looking on from the shore in fits of laughter.

Mr. Haskett's waking dreams that night were almost as confused. He was convinced that Miss Frankland was laboring under a mistake concerning

the identity of Lawrence Conway. Who had told her
he was insane, and was it malice or misunderstanding
on the part of that person? He knew that by a sys-
tem of cross-examination he might, perhaps, light on
the facts of the case. At least he could do his share
toward righting the mistake. But did he want it
rectified? In his inmost heart he thought not. This
absurd muddle, whatever it was, would not injure
Conway in the least, eventually; and as long as Miss
Frankland was afraid of Conway, it left her all the
more time and attention to devote to Conway's friend.
Mr. Haskett was obliged to stay, probably a fortnight,
at the *Hôtel des Salines*, to meet an aunt and cousin
who were to stop there for a day on their return from
the Italian lakes; after which he was to escort them
back to England. During that time he expected to
be much bored. If he could amuse himself by flirting
with this very charming girl, who seemed so ready to
fall in love with him, why should he not? It would
be a temporary softness, of course, but a very agreeable pastime. Perhaps it was a little dishonorable to
his friend to let the mistake run on, but it would
finish in a laugh all round. Possibly he was mistaken
himself about the pretty Miss Frankland. He had
known her such a short time,—she might be the vic-
tim of strange flights of imagination, after all. He

saw plainly that she and Lawrence were quite prepared to fall in love with each other if their con-
sciences would permit. Should he take the blind
from their eyes only to find himself shut out in the
cold, with the remainder of his time heavy on his
hands? No, it would be the height of folly to break
up the amusing delusion yet. So much absurdity
might still arise, and it would be such a capital joke
to laugh over with Conway afterward. "I will let
things rest as they are for a few days longer. Of
course I will not go away and leave them at cross-
purposes. When I am gone they can make eyes at
each other as much as they please; but I don't want
to see them do it, and the only way to prevent that is
to keep up their distrust of each other. I suppose an
explanation will come out of itself in a little while.
It is really one of the best jokes I ever heard. I can't
understand why Conway thinks the young lady half-
witted. But I suppose no girl can be natural when
talking to a lunatic. The old lady, her mother, seems
to be on nettles when Conway is present. By Jove,
what humbugs people are!"

Mr. Haskett's lips parted in a joyless kind of smile,
that seemed more intended to display the faultless
rows of white teeth than to express pleasure.

"Miss Frankland is really a very pleasing girl. It

is best usually to steer clear of the traveling public one meets at continental hotels, but I know these people are well connected. Miss Frankland has all the breeding, without the stiff reserve, of an English gentlewoman. I might have selected a worse spot than the *Hôtel des Salines* for my fortnight's sojourn."

Mr. Haskett's meditations were temporarily interrupted by the process of falling asleep, but they continued, in his dreams, with full vigor; and when he awoke in the morning it was with the fixed resolve to keep his secret as long as possible.

As Mr. Haskett's elaborate and, to himself, highly satisfactory toilette was almost finished, a tap was heard at the door, followed immediately by the entrance of Lawrence Conway.

"Good morning, old chap!" he said cheerfully, "how are you after your ducking?"

"I'm all right this morning, thank you, and, judging by appearances"—applying dexterously some scented pomade to his mustache—"I should say you were in the same felicitous state."

"But you seemed rather the worse for it last night, Haskett."

"I wasn't quite up to the mark yesterday, I admit; though of course I should have rescued Miss Frankland if I had not seen you bent on being the hero of the adventure. She insisted on our going fast, and our coming to grief on that cursed stone was the result. I wonder how she feels after it?"

"You need not feel down in the mouth about the accident, Haskett. I sent up this morning to inquire about Miss Frankland. She is not a bit the worse for it, and will probably be out to-day. By the way, what do you think of her? You seem to have made a very favorable impression. How did she strike you?"

"She certainly is unlike other girls. If one could forget what she was saying, and only watch her as she talked, she would be a delightful companion."

"That's my idea exactly. I am sorry you have come to the same conclusion. I hoped I might have been in fault myself, in some way. Ridiculous mistakes of that kind have happened, you know; but if you think her insane too, I suppose there is no more to be said on the subject. It is a deuced shame! Haskett, would you like a walk to St. Maurice this afternoon? There's a cave or some kind of a hole to be seen there. It is only an hour's walk."

"Not this afternoon, thank you,—it's too hot."

"You are lazier than you used to be."

"And you, much more energetic. I came to this sleepy little place to rest, and, for a day or two, am not going to look at anything — if it's all the same to you."

"Certainly; suit yourself by all means. Only I don't want you to put me down on the invalid list, and therefore unfit for exertion."

Lawrence put his hands in his pockets — an action most soothing to the American mind — and straggled aimlessly about the room, wondering if his friend were ever going to finish his personal adornment; but as that gentleman appeared to engross himself more and more in the arrangement of his hair, Lawrence grew tired of waiting, and took his departure alone.

"When the curls are sufficiently brushed, you will find me down on the terrace," he said, as he closed the door.

"I will join you there in ten minutes," replied Haskett; adding, to himself, "Confound his impertinence! he need not have come bothering here while I was dressing, though the morning is pretty well advanced."

CHAPTER VIII.

IN WHICH OUR HERO REFUSES TO BE REASON-ABLE.

MRS. FRANKLAND is sitting in the drawing-room alone, with her lace-work in hand, but her mind is too much occupied to do justice to fancy work. She is very much troubled at the turn things seem to be taking between her daughter and Count Lemanski. She has observed his way of being present wherever Emily happens to be, and his desire on all occasions to give her a favorable impression of himself. She is also displeased with Emily; she has not at all kept up that dignified coldness toward the Count which she (her mother) approved of so highly at the beginning. No, Emily was now altogether too affable and friendly toward him, and if her encouragement did not cease, he might be emboldened to say or do something dreadful, — perhaps make love to her daughter. Oh, horrors! Fancy a raving lunatic lover slamming himself down on his knees, clawing the air, and pulling out his hair by handfuls! How shocked Emily would be if this should happen! "I can't see any way to prevent them seeing each other unless we go away, and that would be very disagreeable.   We are so comfortable here,—the air suits Emily exactly, she never looked better in her life, and it is so unpleasant to travel in hot weather. It is really very perplexing to know what to do."

The secret of Mrs. Frankland's trouble was the consciousness of her want of control over her daughter.   Emily was very affectionate, and obedient as far as it suited her inclinations to be so; but she had much the stronger will of the two, together with the brightest intellect and clearest insight into other people's characters.   She listened to her mother's exhortations with respectful attention, but afterward used her own judgment about how much it was necessary to obey; and she rarely went astray, for Mrs. Frankland's timid warnings and commands were often so much waste of breath.   She (Mrs. Frankland) had long been used to this state of things, and was never disturbed by Emily's partial disobedience.   But in this instance she was astonished at Emily's lack of common-sense, and longed for a will of iron, to bring her daughter to her way of thinking.

"That accident yesterday has made things much worse.   He came to the rescue very bravely, and civility demands that he should seem grateful.   One

cannot turn the cold shoulder directly after receiving
such a favor. I wish it had been any one else that
had dragged Emily out of the water — one of the men
about the grounds, for instance; one could have
paid him liberally, and that would have been the end
of it. It was very unfortunate that Mr. Haskett himself was not able to save her. Such an adventure is
often the beginning of a devotion that lasts for life.
It seems impossible to know how to treat this crazy
hero, Count Lemanski."

"Good morning, Mrs. Frankland. I was very glad
to hear that Miss Frankland has felt no bad effects
from the accident yesterday."

"Yes, a beautiful morning, thank you — I mean —
What did you say? I beg your pardon," stammered
Mrs. Frankland, much discomfited at the sudden
appearance of the man who of all others she least
wished to see. Lawrence had stepped in at one of
the long windows, and confronted her before she
noticed who he was.

"I said I was pleased to hear that your daughter
was not suffering any inconvenience from her bath in
the lake yesterday. It was much too sudden to be
agreeable."

"Thank you, she seems well this morning, but I
was very much alarmed last night. How can I thank

you enough, Count Lemanski, for your bravery and presence of mind yesterday?"

"Pray don't mention it, Mrs. Frankland. I was delighted to be of some use. The dip in the lake was only so much amusement for me, though I fear it was hardly a diversion to Miss Frankland."

"Indeed, it was not; Emily was quite upset by it," answered Mrs. Frankland, innocent of the pun.

"Are you here for your daughter's health, Mrs. Frankland?"

"Partly," answered that lady, dryly, as she considered the question rather unnecessary.

"Do you not find her much improved since her arrival here?" Lawrence longed to pursue the subject, and find out how serious a malady Miss Frankland's was, but he was afraid of hurting the mother's feelings.

"She is not in need of physical improvement," the lady answered. "I wish I could say the same of her mind; she is very unmanageable sometimes, and I have so little control over her." Mrs. Frankland's outspoken thoughts filled Lawrence with a vague sorrow.

"I am glad the old lady is not disposed to be reserved about her daughter's case. I am afraid, from what she says, that it is more serious than I supposed."

"Has your daughter been a source of trouble to you long, Mrs. Frankland, or is it only temporary?"

"That is an odd question to ask a mother," she said, with an unwilling smile.

"She makes astonishingly light of it," Lawrence thought; "but I suppose it is the best way,—it saves her a heap of unhappiness."

"Has it ever been necessary to keep her under any kind of restraint?" he asked.

"Often it would have been better, I am afraid; but she is an only child, and I have perhaps been over-indulgent."

"I suppose few people notice the difference between her and other young ladies?"

"She is not like other girls," answered Mrs. Frankland, mentally conning over a long list of young ladies of her acquaintance, who were patterns of obedience and docility. "But then," she continued, her maternal pride reasserting itself, "there are few I should care to have her like."

"She certainly is one to eclipse ordinary young ladies wherever she goes, by her interesting peculiarity, aside from her great beauty."

"People are struck with her altogether too much sometimes," said Mrs. Frankland, with feeling.

"Was she born so?"

"Born how?" asked Mrs. Frankland, much bewildered.

"With the failing of which we have been speaking?"

"Oh yes, she has had her own way ever since she
was a child. I suppose I ought to have been more
severe with her." Mrs.. Frankland wondered why
the young man seemed to take such a fatherly interest in the training of her daughter, but attributed
it to his deranged mind.

"Mrs. Frankland, you are alone here,—at least
there is no man to whom you could look for help in
case of necessity."

"Pray, for what cause am I likely to need help?"

"I was going to ask," continued Lawrence, in the
most deferential of tones, "that if your daughter
should become worse and you should need any assistance, you would consider me as a friend ready and
willing to offer any aid in my power?"

"Thank you, but I am quite able to take care of
my daughter myself," answered Mrs. Frankland, very
stiffly. "I suppose it would be undignified," she said
to herself, "to quarrel with the poor half-witted creature, but he certainly is most officious."

"The old lady doesn't accept my offer in the spirit
in which it was made, but her trouble has probably
made her irritable, I must not lay it up against her."

"I am glad to hear she is so little trouble," he said; "she is usually so bright and intelligent, few people would mistrust that her mind was deranged."

All at once the light strikes Mrs. Frankland. She had heard of blind people insisting that none of their fellow-creatures could see. Here was a similar case of a poor lunatic finding his malady reflected in everybody else. He was with Emily more than with the other people, and he had become possessed with the idea that she was insane, and this explained his strange conversation of the past ten minutes.

"I will not undeceive him," she thought, "perhaps he will not haunt her so persistently after this, if he is allowed to believe that she is out of her mind."

This idea had a softening effect on Mrs. Frankland, and she said very cordially: "You are very good to say so, Count Lemanski, and if my daughter should become worse I shall certainly come to you for assistance."

"The old lady is rather capricious, too,— a flighty family, I am afraid."

"Beautiful weather we are having, are we not, Count Lemanski?"

"It is all that could be desired. Mrs. Frankland, permit me to tell you that you have mistaken my name. It is only one of your daughter's whims to call me Count Lemanski."

"But if it does not annoy you I will continue to call you by that name, it is more familiar than any other you could suggest."

Mrs. Frankland had the same objection that her daughter had on a former occasion, to his wandering off on a list of fictitious names.

"She is a little weak in the head, too; there is no doubt about it," said Lawrence, holding open the door for Mrs. Frankland, who had risen, saying she must go to see if her daughter was in need of anything, and resolving mentally to try and prevail on Emily to spend the day in bed. But she arrived too late; during her absence Emily had dressed and gone out on the lawn, where (well for Mrs. Frankland's peace of mind that she did not know it) Lawrence spied and joined her ten minutes after that good lady's departure.

"Good-morning, Miss Frankland," he said; "I am delighted to see you looking so well."

"I was looking for you, Count Lemanski, to thank you for — I can't say saving my life, I was not enough overcome for that, — but for your very timely aid."

"Miss Emily, your mother has just been expressing her gratitude. I will never fish anybody out of the water again if I am to be so overwhelmed with thanks after it."

"Then, for the sake of future unfortunates, I will say no more about it. Wouldn't I be a hard subject to drown if anyone were to try? I wasn't even faint when you lifted me into the boat. I quite spoiled the romance of the adventure."

"But you were the kind of heroine that gives very little trouble, and saves people a great deal of fright."

"I'm sure Mr. Haskett and I both gave trouble enough. How is he this morning? I have not seen him."

"He is quite well, and is probably downstairs by this time."

"Are you sure you are none the worse for your plunge, Count Lemanski?"

"Of course not. My only unpleasant sensation was the fear that you might be indisposed, but that is at rest now."

"Mr. Haskett seemed to take leave of his senses yesterday when the boat went over."

Lawrence took a guilty pleasure in the thought that she perhaps compared Haskett's conduct unfavorably with his own. This permitted him to be magnanimous, so he said:

"Haskett is a very fair sort of fellow, after all

When I saw him this morning he told me he had
been feeling quite out of sorts all day yesterday.   He
is not lacking in bravery."

"Perhaps not; but how about his presence of
mind, which is of more importance?"

It pleased the depraved Lawrence still more to see
that Emily did not incline to adopt his favorable
opinion of his friend.

The two wandered on over the daisy-starred turf;
Emily, with her golden hair, and white dress, seeming not unlike the flowers her dainty little foot was
crushing.   In spite of the virtuous resolve these foolish children had made, not to fall in love with each
other, there were never two pairs of eyes full of more
intense admiration, or two beings more wholly engrossed with each other, than these two, on this
bright morning.

Emily's grateful admiration for Lawrence had, for
the time being, completely transformed her.   She had
none of that air of anxious reserve usual with her
when in his presence, but was perfectly natural, and
talked and laughed in a half bantering, half tender
way, that drove poor Lawrence almost to the verge of
casting prudence to the winds, by falling at those
pretty feet and telling her how he loved her.   But
he restrained himself, and walked by her side in a

kind of blissful intoxication. After all, what did it matter if she were sometimes unlike other women? It made her all the more charming in his eyes. He wanted her for himself, not to please other people. It seemed idiocy to hesitate. He would speak and tell her his love. But then, what kind of an answer could he expect? Only yesterday she had coldly refused to go with him in the boat, and five minutes after had gone, under his very eyes, to the spot he had suggested, with another man. That man was that insinuating flirt, Haskett,—the deuce take him! No, he could not hazard his happiness yet. Besides, he would probably repent it the next moment, if he should ask her to marry him. The summer was long, and he would try to be more certain of himself, and her, before he spoke. He felt that he had already won her esteem, if nothing more.

The change in Emily, of course, made Lawrence appear more in his true light than he had ever done before, and Emily began half to believe that her mother was right after all, and that her peace of mind might be disturbed by this handsome lunatic.

As they were rambling on, a vigorous gale of wind arose.

"Oh, how far we are from home!" exclaimed Emily, looking back with a nervous start.

"I hope you are not tired, Miss Frankland. The way seemed so short to me. I selfishly forgot what it might be to you."

"No, I am not tired in the least; but I think there must be a storm coming up,— the wind is quite furious."

"It will not be any worse than it is now, and this will soon blow over, and then we will go back. I dare not keep you out any longer."

"Yes, we must go home. Mamma will be shocked at my wandering so far alone without somebody along to play propriety."

"Lean against this tree, Miss Frankland. It will protect you from the wind."

As he spoke, a playful gust blew one of Emily's disheveled curls across his breast.

"Oh dear, I am losing all my hair-pins!" she cried, gathering the remaining hair into a loose knot on top of her head, from where it soon fell rippling down, as she tugged at the stray curl to bring it within bounds.

"Wait a moment, Miss Frankland, it has caught around this button,— you will hurt yourself." Lawrence made a poor feint and failure to disentangle the pretty hair.

"I must try something else," he said, taking a penknife from his pocket and cutting the curl loose from the button, coolly leaving an inch or two of the silky hair in his own hand, whence it was conveyed for safer keeping to an inner breast pocket.

"Thank you, Count. This is another example of your presence of mind," she said, with a bright smile that gave another stab to Lawrence's deluded heart.

She seemed innocent of his theft; whether she was really, or only pretending, Lawrence could not decide.

When they turned to go back, Emily broke off a spray of jasmine that hung over the path, and fastened it in her belt. In doing so, Lawrence's gift, the water-lilies, flashed through her mind.

"Count Lemanski, will you refuse to be thanked for the lovely flowers you sent me last night?"

"How can I refuse, if you persist?"

"Did you gather them yourself? I was so pleased."

Lawrence wished she had shown her admiration of his flowers by wearing some of them in her hair. She was very fond of adorning herself in that way, and this was the first morning he remembered seeing her wearing no flowers. But he did not give utterance to his thought.

"I thought afterward the lilies would, perhaps, be too suggestive of your unwelcome plunge. I might have chosen more appropriate flowers."

"No, indeed. I would not like any others better.
They are so beautifully arranged, and will keep their
freshness longer than other flowers."

On nearing the house, Emily saw, through the
trees, her mother slowly advancing toward them, as
if in search of somebody. She had evidently not seen
her delinquent daughter; so Emily, seizing Lawrence
by the arm, and pushing him slightly forward, said:
"Go on, straight before you. Don't follow me." She
then turned and quickly disappeared down a winding path which led to the hotel.

Lawrence obeyed half the command. He did not
follow Emily, but instead of going straight ahead, he,
too, avoided Mrs. Frankland, by turning off abruptly
through the trees before she had discovered him.

When Lawrence was left alone, he began to think
that he had been a hot-headed fool to let himself become so enamored of this pretty English girl. All
her sweet, bewitching ways, and her beauty of form
and feature, were overshadowed by the sad fact that
she was insane. Even before her mother had con-
fided in him, Lawrence could not persuade himself
that she was not. He really must be more reasonable, or else go away. And strange as it may seem,
he had not now the slightest wish to leave the *Hôtel
des Salines.*

CHAPTER IX.

VERA MAKES AN IMPORTANT DISCOVERY.

IN a retired corner of the *Hôtel des Salines* was a complete little apartment of three rooms, situated on that elevation which is called the *entre-sol*, being midway between the ground floor and the first story. The larger of these rooms, which was furnished as a sitting-room, looked out on a little paved court, surrounded on two sides by vine-covered stone walls; the other sides being filled in by the brick walls of the next building.

There was none of the tasteful decoration and ornament which was lavished on other parts of the hotel visible in this quiet little spot, but in its simple neatness and order it had an attraction of its own, which betokened anything but neglect. There was a high, wooden plant-stand, in the form of steps, under the sitting-room window; a few flower-pots on one of the lower shelves. The stand was pushed up against a heavy, clinging ivy, whose ancient, wooded arms and dark, thick leaves, had taken the whole side of the house in its strong embrace. The windows of

these three little rooms were curiously seamed from
top to bottom with slender white bars, which any one,
examining closely, would have discovered to be of
solid iron, painted white.   The outside approach to
this court was through a small, dark passage, branch-
ing off from the stone archway that formed the entrance to the stables.

The guests of the hotel were, of course, never
seen in these obscure regions, and if any one had
noticed the little white-robed figure that stole noiselessly under the archway, with eyes wide with astonishment to find herself in unexplored ground, she
would have been taken back, without ceremony,
to the brighter side of the picture, where she belonged.   But no one noticed her, and Vera, leaving
the arched gate, peered cautiously into the narrow
passage.   She saw light at the other end, and, half
hesitating and wholly curious, she ventured in, and
soon found herself in the quiet little court already
described.   She wandered about the enclosure, and,
finding nothing there to interest her, was turning to come away again, when a peal of laughter
behind the iron bars startled her and riveted her
attention.   This was repeated again and again, accompanied by the crashing of broken glass.   Vera's
curiosity was all excited; she forgot her alarm and

her usual politeness, and climbed to the top of the flower-stand. From the top of this it seemed such a little distance to where the sound came from, that she made a ladder of the thick, twining ivy trunk, and drew herself up till her head was on a level with the window-sill. Six inches higher, and her big, startled blue eyes were peering into the room, and, with her little fingers tightly clutching the iron bars, she watched, unobserved, a grotesque game of nine-pins that was going on within.

A pale young man, with wild, dark eyes and long, straggling, black hair,—attired in a red and black dressing-gown, with an embroidered slipper on one foot and a torn silk stocking on the other,—was sitting on the floor opposite nine wine-bottles in various stages of demolition, standing in a row, into whose midst he sent spinning a loaf of brown bread.

Every stroke told with startling effect. The bottles fell over with a crash,—some of them, half full,—pouring their contents in streams among the bits of broken glass. After every stroke the eccentric player set up a shout of childish laughter, writhing himself to and fro in his delight, and then, scrambling on all-fours to recover the bread and set up the remaining bottles, took his position for another shot.

Vera watched this pastime in amazement, till she
felt her tired fingers relaxing their hold of the bars
and she was forced to let herself down to the ground
again.

"That was the poor crazy young man mamma
was speaking of; but she told me I must not talk
about him. I will not tell her I have seen him,—
she might be angry," she said to herself.

When she reached the ground, she saw with dis-
may the dreadful destruction of her white dress and
slippers. "Oh *mon Dieu!* what will Annette say?
Tant pis! it is nothing. When I come again I
will speak to the young man. Perhaps he would
like to have some one to play with him."

Mr. Conway took a long walk alone that afternoon,
and on his return found two letters awaiting him,—
one from his mother, full of anxious inquiry about
his health, the other from his banker in Geneva, re-
questing his immediate presence there on business.
A week ago Lawrence would have hailed with delight
any cause that would remove him from the *Hôtel des
Salines.* Now that it seemed expedient in more ways
than one, he was most unwilling to go, and as he
re-read his letter he consigned Geneva bankers in
general to a very warm locality. He tried to cheat
himself with the thought that it was Haskett's pres-

ence that made his stay at the hotel more agreeable; but after all, he and Haskett were very little together. There was no denying the fact that this golden-haired girl was taking possession of him, heart and soul. He might reason with himself and take a common-sense view of the case twenty times a day, but in her presence he always found himself forgetting her eccentricities, and seeing in her only a wonderfully fair, seductive woman, whom he could fall down and worship.

He knew he was wandering in a fool's paradise, but he did not want to grow wise yet, and this Geneva letter was a rude interruption to his idle dreaming.

Mr. Haskett walked down to the station the next morning with Lawrence, as he went to take the train for Geneva.

"Are there any errands I could do for you in town, Haskett?"

"No, thank you; I shall be going that way myself before long. When will you be back?"

"I shall not be away more than a couple of days."

"Does any one know you are going?"

"No. Give my compliments to Miss Frankland, and tell her I hoped to say good-bye, but my train goes too early."

" I hope your affairs will turn out all right."

" Oh, there's nothing wrong, I imagine. I'm off now,— good-bye, Haskett." Lawrence shook hands with his friend through the railway carriage window, and was out of sight in a moment.

As Mr. Haskett walked back alone he felt a certain sense of satisfaction. He had let the deception go on so long now that it would be really very awkward if the discovery came about before he intended it should. The deceived pair might not, perhaps, view it in the light of a joke. Miss Frankland might be offended, and he so particularly wished that young lady to have a good opinion of him. The fact was, Mr. Haskett, after much consideration, had made up his mind to propose to Emily Frankland. It was hardly probable that she would refuse such a very advantageous offer; and if the little misunderstanding about Lawrence should be brought to light inadvertently, the part he had played in it would be forgiven in an accepted lover. But he meant to do his best to keep the mystery from being cleared up,— at least, while they were all together there. It would not be such a difficult thing to do. The four people most concerned mixed very little with the other boarders, so there was little danger to be apprehended from them; three of these people had not the least suspicion of any mistake, and he, the fourth, was certainly not going to excite their suspicion. There was that chattering child, Vera, who might bring about an explanation, but no one attended, however, to what she said, fortunately. He (Haskett) was only to be at the hotel about a week longer. Two dangerous days were tided over by Conway's absence. The Franklands would not be staying much longer, and Conway himself would leave soon. Conway was a good enough sort of fellow, but Mr. Haskett never once thought of him when he was out of sight, and, married and settled in his home in Surrey, he would never hear of him again, unless, perhaps, his wife might sometimes speak in a compassionate tone of Count Lemanski! Fortune had favored him wonderfully so far,—he would be very dull if he had not Emily's heart in his own keeping before she discovered that it was not folly to admire Conway. But she was not going to discover anything of the kind——

A flower woman presenting her basket for his inspection interrupted the current of his thoughts.

"Where did you get such fine gentians, my good woman? It is early for them."

"High up, monsieur, on the *Dent du Midi.*"

"Was it much of a climb?"

"Not much for me, but monsieur could not do it."

"Haven't you seen enough of English people yet to know that they can walk anywhere?"

"Is monsieur English? I am astonished; monsieur speaks French so well, one would not suppose it."

"You expect an extra franc for that compliment, do you not?"

"It is as monsieur pleases."

"Make me up a nice bunch of gentians and wild roses. You need not mix in any garden flowers; I can get plenty of them at the hotel."

"Monsieur will take myosotis for the lady?"

"How do you know they are for a lady, *bavarde?*"

"Monsieur would not buy roses for himself."

"When you can get any *edelweiss* bring it to me. I want to send some to my friends in England. Do you hear?"

"Monsieur is very amiable. I will not forget."

"Put in some more of those white buds. There, that will do. There is something to buy a pair of shoe-buckles."

The woman extricated the five-franc piece from the loose flowers in her basket, reciting a fervent prayer for the generous stranger, while Mr. Haskett continued his way to the hotel. As he entered the grounds he met the object of his thoughts, Emily Frankland.

"You return early from your walk, Mr. Haskett. Have you been far?"

"Far enough to find these flowers. Do you think them worth accepting, Miss Frankland? I got them for you."

"Did you take the trouble to gather these,—and for me? I feel very much flattered. It is not easy to find gentians about here unless one is a very energetic climber. I did not think you cared much for that kind of exertion."

"You think I am very indolent, lazy and generally good for nothing, do you, Miss Emily?"

"Certainly not; I never thought so, and if I had I would have to change my opinion now."

"I wish all my faults in your eyes could be cleared up as easily."

"But I have not been condemning you for anything; what do you mean?"

"Oh, nothing,—I was only dreaming; but I had rather you found fault with me than not think of me at all."

There was a soft look in his usually steel-like blue eyes as he said this, which was easy to interpret, and Emily felt her voice tremble slightly as she said:

"I have a piece of news to tell you, Mr. Haskett."

"Indeed! What is it?"

"There is to be a grand ball given here next Thursday."

" In the village, do you mean ? "

" No, here at the *Salines*. Doesn't that interest you ? "

" Very much, if I am here on that evening."

" But you are not thinking of going away, Mr. Haskett ? "

" I was thinking of it. My plans will not permit me to stay much longer; otherwise I should not think of leaving for a long time yet. It is very delightful here."

"But you must stay till after the ball."

" Do you want me to stay ? "

" Why, yes, of course. There are so few gentlemen who dance well, that it is the duty ——"

" Is that the only reason why you want me to stay, so that I can offer my services for the general good, as the musicians and other ball-room furniture offer theirs ? "

" If I say there are other reasons why I want you to be at the ball, will you stay ? "

" I will, Miss Emily, let the consequences be what they may."

"If you talk so seriously I shall insist on your going. It is just possible that the gossips have said
more than is true about the ball, but I think it certainly will come off on Thursday."

"It is no more than ought to be done for the diversion of the pilgrims here. By the way, Mr. Con——"

Just in time the speaker bethought himself; he
had almost spoken his friend's name. Furthermore, if
he mentioned the fact, even, of Count Lemanski having gone to Geneva alone, it would excite comment.
He would trust to luck to have his absence explained
some other way, so Conway's message to Miss Frankland should not be conveyed, and he would say nothing about his departure.

"What were you going to say, Mr. Haskett? You
did not finish your sentence."

"I was going to say that Mr. Campbell, the light-
haired Scotchman, seemed to be a tolerable dancer."

"Yes, he is not bad. Why don't you honor our
little dances in the back drawing-room with your
presence more, Mr. Haskett? You came once, to
show us how well you could dance, and then deserted
us."

"Dancing, for the sake of dancing, I never enjoy;
it is a giddy, unpleasant exercise. But in a handsome ball-room, radiant with wax tapers and brilliant

costumes, with intoxicating music to stir one's blood, dancing becomes a pleasure, especially if there are good wines and edibles to refresh one afterward. I detest an impromptu dance, with somebody grinding spasmodic waltzes out of an ill-used piano. The game is not worth the candle."

"I am afraid the ball here will not be grand enough to suit you, Mr. Haskett."

"I shall not forget that it is an effort on the part of a landlord to please a miscellaneous public, and I will not be too critical."

At a turn in the avenue Emily and her companion met Vera walking with her little brother, and Annette. The child left the nurse and baby, and ran forward to meet Emily, enthusiastically admiring her flowers.

"Mr. Haskett has given them to you, *n'est-ce-pas*, Miss Emily?"

"Yes, Mr. Haskett has been so kind."

"I saw a woman with such flowers in a basket — did you bought them of she, Mr. Haskett?"

"Vera, you are altogether too inquisitive," he said, less angry than he would have been had he not seen that Emily's attention was engrossed by the son and heir of Madame von Kolatschewski, and she had not heard Vera's remark.

"Oh, Mr. Haskett, I see such a funny thing yesterday. I have not said it to no one, for I cannot find Mr. Conway; but I went on a vine, high up to a window, and such a man with long hairs, and eyes like crazy stars, was rolling hisself on the carpet, and kicking bottles with a bread. He is a poor crazy gentleman, I heard my mamma tell some lady; his name is Count Lemanski."

"What does she say about Count Lemanski?" Emily asked, attracted by the name, and permitting the nurse and baby to continue their walk.

"Vera talks too much for a little girl," answered Mr. Haskett hastily, before the child had time to speak again; "she had much better go and play with the other children than to spend so much time chattering with older people. Do you see your nurse is getting almost out of sight? Run after her or you will have to go home alone."

Vera, much hurt and astonished at her dismissal, and the cold reception of her absorbing story, obeyed without a word, giving one disdainful glance at her oppressor.

"You are not fond of children, I see, Mr. Haskett," Emily said, as soon as the little girl was out of hearing.

"I am quite indifferent to children usually, but

I can't endure that child," Mr. Haskett answered, more angrily than he intended to. "She is so forward, and vain."

"She is forward in one sense,—her intellect is far ahead of. her years. As for her vanity, I think she has wonderfully little, considering every one admires her without reserve. She never makes herself noticeable unless some one encourages her to talk. Most people delight in her quaint sayings."

"The way she muddles up her English is sometimes amusing."

"She is just as odd when she talks other languages. I think she is a wonderfully good child, considering all the spoiling influences against her."

"I believe strongly in the old saying that children should be seen, and not heard." There was an unpleasant expression on Mr. Haskett's face, caused by the revelation just made. The truth had flashed across him as Vera finished her story. There was, confined somewhere in the hotel, a lunatic by the name of Lemanski, with whom, by some misconception, Emily and her mother had identified Lawrence Conway. Mr. Haskett had long suspected the existence of some such person, and now this chattering little girl had enlightened him. She was the last person in the world whom he would have chosen to make the discovery, for of course she would tell her story to Miss Frankland, and then the murder would be out. Miss Frankland was so absurdly fond of the child, he wished he could contrive some way of keeping the two separated, but nothing occurred to him. Perhaps he could frighten Vera out of telling her secret to any one else. It was really becoming vexatious to keep up this ridiculous hoax any longer, but it would not do to have the explanation come yet. In his cold, calculating way, Sidney Haskett loved, as well as admired, the girl he meant to ask to be his wife, and the thought of another man stepping in and bearing off the prize, that was so nearly within his grasp, was gall and bitterness to him.

"I believe I'll find out some more about that crazy fellow from the little white-frilled humbug," he said to himself, as Miss Frankland took leave of him at the foot of the stairs. Vera, who was never hard to find, was discovered on a little balcony off the dining-room.

"Where did you see the strange young man, you were telling me about, Vera?" asked Mr. Haskett, coming out on the balcony with a cigar in his mouth.

Vera had not forgotten his manner when she

last saw him, and she was not disposed to be confidential again.

"It was far away,—you could not go there," she said.

"Will you tell me where it was?"

"No, you would break the flower steps."

"Just as you like, Vera,—but if I were you, I would not tell any one you had seen this young man."

"My mamma said me not to speak of him,—but I will tell only Miss Emily, and Mr. Conway."

"I think you had better not."

"Why for?"

"Because they would think you were a prying, inquisitive little girl. Do you understand that?"

"No."

"It means something very bad. When any one is ill, like that poor young man, people don't talk about him. Mr. Conway and Miss Emily would be shocked to hear it."

"And cross like a bear? You were when I told you,—but they are good, and not never cross. Do you see that little bird-nest on the vine up there?"

"Yes,—do you want it?"

"You are not long enough,—you can't reach to it."

"Yes, I can," he said, stretching up and detaching the nest with some difficulty. "Now, Vera, we are friends again, are we not?" he said, handing her the nest.

"As much as always," the child answered.

When he had gone, she threw the nest over the balcony railing. "Why does that man scold me, and look angry, when other people are kind? The nest makes me think of him. I would rather think of some one else."

CHAPTER X.

WHAT WAS IN A BOTTLE.

MR. CONWAY'S visit to Geneva was uneventful and uninteresting in the extreme, except for one little transaction at the jewelry establishment of Messieurs Patek and Philip, on the *Grand Quai*. He left there a little curl of soft, fair hair, to be made into a ring of fit proportions, to fit the little finger of his own left hand. It would be a souvenir of a few of the brightest hours of his life, he said to himself,—"a fellow don't have so much happiness in this world that he can afford to forget any of it."

His more common-place errands, connected with various banks, occupied more time than he had supposed necessary, and it was not till three days after his departure that he was able to return to Bex.

He arrived at the *Grand Hôtel des Salines* about three o'clock in the afternoon. It was a beautiful day, and most of the guests who could accomplish it had taken advantage of the fine, cool weather, and gone on an excursion of pleasure, or annoyance, according to companions chosen.

There was, however, one little bright-eyed damsel left to give the wanderer a welcome, and Vera's exuberant delight at seeing him again atoned in a great measure for the absence of other friends.

"Oh, Mr. Conway, I have been *désolée* since you go away! Where did you went, and why did you not take me too?" she said, putting her mite of a hand in his.

"I would have taken you if I had thought you wanted to go. I had a lonely kind of a time in Geneva."

"What did you make in Geneva?"

"I didn't do anything that would interest you. I saw such fine shops, diamonds and beautiful things; enough to bury a little girl like you so deep that no one could ever find her again."

"I have been in Geneva. It is nice."

"Do you like to open bundles, Vera, and find things inside for yourself?"

"Oh yes!"

"Well, open that, and see if you like it," he said, taking a mysterious looking bundle from his satchel.

"Why did you bring to me an ugly black bottle?" asked Vera, when she had opened the bundle, looking up at him with a half amused, half disappointed smile. "Is there anything in it?"

"Set it down on the ground and see."

She obeyed; whereupon was heard issuing from the bowels of the bottle a lively air from *"La Fille de Madame Angot,"* followed by half a dozen other favorite melodies. Then, with much grunting and quivering, the musical bottle relapsed again into unattractive silence.

"Oh, *mon Dieu!* what a lovely singing angel, for a black bottle! Is it for me, *vraiment?* I am so obliged. And I said it was ugly!" she said, hugging the squatty, vulgar looking bottle up to her bosom.

"Now I can make scare everybody. Oh *ciel!* but that will be a—fun!"

"Where are all the other people, Vera?"

"I don't know."

"Why are you not out with Miss Emily? She usually likes to have you with her."

"Miss Emily and Mr. Haskett have gone walking in a carriage."

"Does Miss Emily like Mr. Haskett?"

"Oh yes; she make sweet eyes at him, and is glad when he comes. I don't like Mr. Haskett."

"Why not?"

"He has got some bad, wicked eyes. He tells me to go to play with the children, and his eyes say, 'Go to the devil!'"

"Why, Vera, little girls don't swear in English! I am quite shocked."

"Was that a swear? Miss Hammond tell me something about what was 'to swear,' but I have not much understand. Must I not say 'damned swindle?'"

"You little reprobate! where did you learn such bad words?"

"I have heard many gentlemen say them.'

"That is no reason why you should. You must forget your 'swears' as soon as possible, and never say any of them again."

"Mr. Conway, why does Miss Emily wear the flowers Mr. Haskett give her in her hair, and not wear the pretty lilies you send?"

"I suppose she likes Mr. Haskett's flowers best."

"When she was in her bed the night she fell out of the boat, I made her beautiful with the lilies in her hair. I would go to bring you to admire, but she said me that she did not want you to know that English ladies went in beds. Does she like Mr. Haskett best? You are much nicer. Why don't she like you more?"

"My dear child, you are altogether too much of a catechist. How can I answer all your questions?"

Lawrence answered with a laugh; but the child's prattle had raised a feeling very akin to jealousy in his heart. Of course he was not going to trust too much to the chatter of a child, but was Haskett serious in his attentions to Miss Frankland? It seemed hardly possible with his fastidious ideas. Could he be so reckless as to beguile her into loving him? It might be the finishing touch to overthrow her unbalanced mind, when he went away. "I believe I will ask him what he means. I introduced him, and should never forgive myself if he turned out a scamp."

"What are you thinking of, Mr. Conway? You look so *triste*."

"I was thinking how hungry I was, Vera, and that if I did not get something to eat in five minutes, I should die, or else find out if little Russian girls were good to eat."

"May I sit with you while you have dinner?"

"Yes, if it would amuse you."

As the oddly matched pair were sitting at a little round table, outside under the trees, Lawrence asked:

"Did Miss Emily and Mr. Haskett go alone in the carriage?"

"Alone, except a man did sit behind. They went in a small, low carriage."

"Then Mrs. Frankland did not go?"

"No, she stood up on the balcony and throw them a shawl, and prayed them not to be out late. There was not place for her in the carriage, I suppose."

"Strange," mused Lawrence, "that her mother should allow her to go out alone with him. I am an American, and there would be nothing unbecoming in her going out alone with me; yet I might ask in vain for such a favor. The fates are certainly against me. I wonder if Haskett is going too far?"

"What have you said, Mr. Conway?" asked a small voice whose existence he had almost forgotten.

"Nothing, Vera. I must take a tender farewell of you now, for I must go and put myself in a salt pickle to get the dust off."

From his window, two hours later, Lawrence watched the return of Miss Frankland and Mr. Haskett from their drive. She was all brightness and smiles, and Lawrence watched his friend with another jealous pang as he handed her out of the carriage. "I wonder if I have been an over-cautious idiot about that girl, or is Haskett daring too much? I will ask him what he means, if I do get myself into a scrape."

"Haskett!" he called from the balcony railing, "come up and have a smoke."

"So you are back again, Conway," Mr. Haskett said, as he came into his room five minutes later, and settled himself in the only easy-chair the room afforded. "What delayed you?"

"One of the confounded fellows I had to see was out of town. I had to wait till he came back."

"Did you find things all straight?"

"Oh, fair enough. Nothing has been going on here, I suppose, since I left?"

"Oh no; we have all been quiet as mice."

"Has Miss Frankland developed any new and startling ideas?"

"Nothing more than usual."

"You have had good opportunity for observation."

"What do you mean?"

"I mean that you and she seem to be having what would be called between sane people quite a flirtation."

When Lawrence dismissed Vera, he had gone to the reading-room, where, in a conversation with Mr. Campbell, the Scotchman, that gentleman had informed him, together with much other gossip, that the people of the hotel generally supposed Miss Frankland and Mr. Haskett to be engaged. He had not put much faith in this alone, but, taken in conjunction with what Vera had said, he felt there was cause for uneasiness.

"It is a fortunate thing we are not sane people," drawled Mr. Haskett, in reply to Lawrence's last remark, as he lazily watched the curls of smoke swaying over his scented locks.

"What would you do, Haskett, if the fair lunatic were to fall in love with you?"

"Return the tender passion, I suppose." ·

"Do you mean to say you would ask a woman to be your wife whom you knew to be half crazy?"

"My dear fellow, what's the use of talking so seriously? Who is going to give a moment's thought to the few soft nothings exchanged between two people who are thrown together for a few days at a hotel? I confess I admire Miss Frankland; she amuses me, as a score of other girls I could mention amuse me."

"But Miss Frankland is not like other girls, you must remember."

"On some subjects she is sharp as a dozen girls. She is not one of the kind that dies of a broken heart. She is such a capricious, unstable little thing, that one would never dream of talking of anything serious with her. But this is absurdity, Conway, to talk of what she is, or is not, with you. You know her quite, as well, and better, than I do. As far as flirtation is concerned, I think we are both in the same boat."

"She never went driving with me alone."

"Did you ever ask her?"

"No, for I knew it would be of no use."

"Going out with me alone counts for nothing here. It could not be done in England; but English people on the continent are much less strict in their ideas."

"There are few English girls who would go out for an afternoon alone with a gentleman, even on the continent, unless they were engaged."

"There you are mistaken, Conway. In a quiet place like this, Mrs. Grundy has very little to say. English girls can be almost as unrestrained as your fair American sisters. Besides, Miss Frankland is very unlike the ordinary English girl."

"I think you forget that too much."

"Conway, I appreciate your motive in speaking, and shall not take exception at what you say. You have heard some of the gossip of the hotel, and want to warn me not to go too far. I beg of you not to trouble yourself with any more of these foolish ideas. I certainly would never marry a lunatic, and I flatter myself I am a man of too much honor to entrap a girl's affections and then throw them away. Miss Frankland is not such a tender, susceptible creature as you think. There is not the slightest cause for uneasiness, no matter what the gossips may say."

Lawrence could not deny that his friend's intentions seemed harmless, but, as he went downstairs, he was conscious of a vexed, dissatisfied feeling which he could not define.

There was some one playing a selection from "*Lohengrin*" in the back drawing-room. Lawrence guessed it was Miss Frankland, and, on entering the room, was not disappointed.

"Oh, Count Lemanski! where have you been all this time? I have not seen you for several days."

"Didn't Haskett give you my message, and tell you I had gone to Geneva?"

"No, he did not give me any message, nor say anything about you. Poor fellow," she said to herself, "I suppose he has been shut up for some misdemeanor for the past few days, and he is trying to account to me for his disappearance. I wonder Mr. Haskett did not tell me anything about him. I never like to ask him about poor Darwin,— he always seems anxious to avoid the subject."

"It is very strange that he did not tell you," continued Lawrence; but then he remembered that Haskett might have told her and she had forgotten all about it the next moment.

"May I have the pleasure of joining you at the music this evening, Miss Frankland?"

"I am afraid that is impossible, as Mr. Haskett is going to take mamma and me boating on the river this evening. We shall not return until the music is over."

"You are going to trust yourself again on the water with him?"

"Yes, I am going to be so daring. Perhaps you will walk along the shore, to be ready, in case of necessity, to offer your assistance," she said with a merry laugh.

"I am afraid Mr. Haskett would think me *de trop*."

A voice outside was heard calling "Emily!"

"Mamma is looking for me, so I must go. Good-bye, Count Lemanski; I shall see you to-morrow." She left the room with a careless nod and smile, while Lawrence sat for a long time on the sofa, a prey to his own gloomy thoughts.

How everything seemed to have changed in the last three or four days! He had gone away living over again the hours passed with Emily, and thinking their delightful rambles and *tête-à-têtes*, in which he was so foolishly happy, and she too seemed pleased, might be repeated over and over again on his return. He was not really in love with her, of course — that could never be; it was more a kindly, brotherly feeling — pity, perhaps. But then pity is akin to love, and in his case the connection was very close. He knew they could not go on wandering about the grounds and smiling into each other's eyes forever. A few short weeks more, and then the dream must end; but perhaps by that time they would have come to their senses, and then the separation would not be so hard. But the end seemed to have come abruptly now, and without having committed any offense Lawrence felt himself cast off and left behind. Haskett, the new-comer, had supplanted him and gained the first place in Emily's thoughts, by a little reck-lessness of possible consequences,— a place that he, Lawrence, might still have occupied if he had not been so stupidly prudent and considerate. He had been fool enough to look forward with pleasure to Haskett's arrival — but what kind of a companion had he been? He had not made any of the trips they had planned together, and never tried to make himself agreeable, except when Miss Frankland was present. It seemed to Lawrence as if these two — Mr. Haskett and Miss Frankland — felt his presence to be a disagreeable restraint. Emily's manner had changed wonderfully toward him since he went to Geneva, and Haskett was, if possible, more indifferent than ever. Perhaps it was only imagination,— at any rate he believed he would try a change; he was get-

ting low-spirited again, and out of sorts generally.
He thought he would go away for a while, and perhaps at the end of ten days or a fortnight there
would be a different set of people at the hotel, and he
would manage to get up an interest in some of them.
He certainly would. not stay here to watch and hear
about the progress of the flirtation between Miss
Frankland and Haskett. On such thoughts intent,
he made his way to Mr. Haskett's room, and found
that gentleman subjecting his finger-nails to a careful
course of pruning. Without desisting from this occupation, he begged Lawrence to be seated.

"How much longer are you going to be here, Haskett? — if I may ask."

"Probably a week longer."

"Then I won't see you when I come back."

"Are you going away again?" Mr. Haskett's face
was not one that often expressed pleasant emotions,
or he would have looked delighted at this suggestion.

"Yes, I am bored to death here. I shall go to
Chamonix, and perhaps take a look at the Holy Barn-
yard, as Johnston calls the St. Bernard monastery."

"I have been to that far-famed place. You will
find it a nice trip if the weather is propitious."

"It will not be very inspiriting, starting out alone
as I do; but I shall of course fall in with somebody

on the way. I suppose you have no desire to leave the *Salines* long enough for a trip to Chamonix, Haskett?"

"I should like to go, very much; but I have got to be on the move so soon with those cousins of mine, that I think I will keep quiet here while I can. Chamonix is very hard work. Conway, there is to be a ball here; do you care anything for that?"

"I care so much that I shall take particular pains to escape it. When is it?"

"Thursday evening."

"That will suit me exactly; I am going Wednesday morning."

"If I shouldn't be here when you come back, you know where you can always find my address,— but I need not give you any parting injunctions yet, I shall see you again before you go." Mr. Haskett was so pleased with Conway for taking himself out of the way so opportunely, that he greatly astonished that gentleman by an overflow of cordiality and amiability up to the hour of his departure.

CHAPTER XI.

A LOSS, ATTENDED WITH MUCH GAIN.

IT was the evening of the ball at the *Hôtel des Salines*. Before the revel grew to its height, a pretty group might have been seen occupying one of the flower-decked ante-rooms. Mrs. Frankland, dressed in a pale gray *moiré antique*, with rich lace gathered about her plump, fair hands, and lying in cloudy folds over her ample bosom, her snowy hair adorned with a graceful fall of the same delicate fabric, held in place by a white camellia surrounded by its dark green leaves, is talking confidentially to Mr. Haskett. He, rigid in swallow-tail and patent leather boots, with immaculate cravat and gloves, is watching the two brightest figures in the scene, sitting on the opposite sofa, apparently engrossed in each other.

Emily, in clouds of white tulle, is like a pure lily. Her dress is caught up at intervals with graceful sprays of myosotis, a treble string of pearls encircles her soft white arms, and another droops low on her lovely neck, and more are twined in her pretty, golden hair. Her companion on the sofa is her little friend Vera, dressed in a richly embroidered white India muslin, stopping just above her bare knees. Her round, rosy legs are bare to the ankle, where her attire begins again with silk stockings and white satin slippers. A broad white sash is tied below her waist, and her pretty light hair, short over the forehead and long behind, is divided by a row of pure white daisies. She is allowed to be at the ball for the first two hours, and her delight knows no bounds.

"No, he will not be permit to come at the ball, Miss Emily."

"Are you sure you saw Count Lemanski shut up in a room with barred windows, Vera?"

"Yes, much times; I go there quite very often. He makes strange things."

"What does he make?"

"He rolls hisself round about — and laughs."

"He *does* strange things, you mean."

"Yes; is not *do* and *make* all same?"

"Not always; but I could never explain the difference to you."

"Will you come and do him a visit, Miss Emily? You could hang your hands to a tree that grimpers on a house; then there are some steps that see into a window."

"Your description is very inviting, Vera, but I do

not want to see the poor young man when he is not
well; you ought not to go there so much, it is not a
proper place for a little girl."

"What are you two talking about so earnestly?"
asked Mr. Haskett.

"Oh, Miss Emily, *je vous prie, ne dites* nothing of
what I tell you! He tell me I must not say nothing!"
Vera exclaimed, seizing Emily's arm with her little
white-gloved hand. Emily was a little astonished at
the child's vehemence as she answered:

"We are talking secrets, you must not interrupt."

"What a wonderful fancy your daughter seems to
have taken to that little coquette of a child," observed
Mr. Haskett to Mrs. Frankland.

"She is an odd little girl. I hope she will not be
spoiled by all the notice she gets. What a lovely little
fairy she is to-night!"

"It is ridiculous, the idea of a baby like that being
allowed to come to a ball; her mother must be insane
to allow it."

As the music of the second waltz struck up, Mr.
Haskett gave his arm to Mrs. Frankland, while Emily
and Vera followed them into the ball-room. There
was less sameness in the appearance of the guests
than in most such entertainments. Persons having
friends stopping at the other hotels in Bex had been

requested to invite them, and the result was an assemblage of people from all the stray corners of civilized Europe and America, and the modes of dancing were varied as the people. Springy, agile Frenchmen were spinning through the waltz, rippling over with smiles and talking incessantly as they danced; Russians, darting like lightning through the thickest of the crowd, with a miraculous power of saving their partners from the slightest graze from the other whirling couples. Dignified Englishmen, plodding steadily ahead, bent on making their way once round the room, indifferent to the number of bumps and collisions encountered on the way. Solemn-visaged Americans, ambling slowly about in retired corners of the room, with their hands resting on each others' shoulders, either for mutual support or to keep each other off, the gentlemen showing a tendency to double up at the knees, as if they found the exercise too severe. Among all the gay throng, the Germans seemed best to appreciate the poetry of dancing; and as they glided swiftly and easily down the long hall, the spectator found himself involuntarily charmed by their graceful movements.

The evening wore on, and an hour after midnight Mr. Haskett and Emily went into the conservatory for a little rest and fresh air.

"Do you ever visit your friend in his prison, Mr. Haskett?" Emily was saying.

No, I never have." He was afraid to commit himself by saying more, not knowing what Emily might have heard.

"It is a great pity he has to be shut up to-night,— I think this gay scene would do him good."

"How did you hear he was shut up, Miss Emily?"

"Vera has discovered in some way the room where he is confined; she saw him to-day. By the way, she told me not to say anything about it to you, so you must not betray me. It is dreadful to think of the poor fellow caged like a wild beast to-day, when only the day before yesterday he was as calm and sane as we are."

"So Vera told you she saw Count Lemanski a prisoner in his barred room. Does ever anything happen here, I wonder, that that child does not know all about?"

"You do not like to have his confinement talked about?"

"Would you, in my place?"

"I am always talking about Count Lemanski, and I know it always annoys you. I *will* speak of something else."

Mr. Haskett was congratulating himself that the

last stumbling-block in his way had been removed —
that *enfant terrible* had done him a great service.
She had kept her secret just long enough, and in telling about Count Lemanski after Lawrence had gone
she accounted for the latter's absence in a most satisfactory way. Mr. Haskett could not have done it
better himself.

"What a bore it is to be always among these crowds
of chattering strangers; do you not often wish yourself back where you heard only your mother tongue,
Miss Emily?"

"No, I find the variety charming, though I wish
some of the scenes in the changing panorama were
more lasting. Probably when I have traveled as
much as you have, Mr. Haskett, I shall think as you
do."

"I believe you are right. I have been away too
long; going home would be very delightful — under
some circumstances."

"Mamma tells me you have a very beautiful home."

"The place is admired, and, I believe, not unjustly;
but the place is dreary and cheerless, as a house without a mistress always is. I have thought of this,
and have often wished my home was brightened by a
woman's presence; but I have never seen the woman
I would call my wife — till now. I will not keep my

secret any longer,—perhaps it is not a secret. I love you, Emily, as I never loved any one before, and if you refuse to be mistress of my heart and home, both will go very long without a tenant."

Emily was not astonished at this disclosure, as she could not help seeing it was impending for several days, but she was not prepared to answer, and only picked nervously at the superb bouquet of flowers Mr. Haskett had given her earlier in the evening.

"You don't answer; but I must give you time. You will not keep me waiting long?"

"Till to-morrow," she answered in a low voice, without looking up.

"Till to-morrow," he repeated, touching her one ungloved hand with his lips, and, drawing it through his arm, conducted her back to the ball-room, from which, an hour afterward, the persons most connected with this history had disappeared.

To return to the fortunes of Lawrence, or misfortunes, as they happen to be in this instance, which were brought about in the following way: On leaving the *Hôtel des Salines* he gave up the idea of stopping off at Martigny (the point from which one proceeds per mule-back to Chamonix), and went on to Saxon instead. Saxon being a miniature Baden-Baden, or

Monaco, and the only place in Switzerland where gaming-tables flourish, Lawrence had great curiosity to see the playing, and of course to try his luck. He played small stakes and won almost incessantly at *rouge-et-noir*, and then, with a dozen or so extra napoleons in his possession, experimented at *roulette*. Here he was not so fortunate; he lost all his winnings and twenty-five napoleons besides. He was then wise enough to stop playing and give up trying to leave off where he had begun, which is the fatal error of most casual gamblers.

With an intense feeling of disgust for gambling-rooms in general, and those of Saxon in particular, he went out into the garden to drink a cup of coffee and cognac, and listen to the music. It was growing dusk as he left the *établissement*, and when he next had occasion to use his purse he found that some pickpocket had relieved him of all his remaining money, except a few francs loose in his pockets that would little more than pay for a room and supper at the hotel. "It was a shabby trick to rob a fellow after he had lost at that confounded table," he said to himself; "if I had won a pile of money there might have been some justice in it."

He reported his loss at a police station, but with very little hope of recovering his money, and taking

a room at the *Hôtel Bellevue,* went to bed, in a rage
with himself and his surroundings. He could not do
otherwise than return ignominiously to Bex the next
day, and wait at the *Hôtel des Salines* till another re-
mittance came from Paris. This thought was most
distasteful to him; he wanted to forget Bex and every one there if he could, and now he was forced back
among them all. Then he would have to account for
his sudden return and find himself the subject of
abominable jokes for days. He would stay in Saxon
till after the ball at the *Salines,* at any rate; he would
not be bored with that, or with questions about his
absence.

CHAPTER XII.

A NEW ACQUAINTANCE.

WHEN Emily went down to breakfast, at eleven o'clock, the morning after the ball, she found the dining-room deserted. She took her place and began her lonely meal, thinking of Mr. Haskett, and what he had said to her last night, and feeling a sense of relief that he was not in the dining-room; for she did not feel courageous enough to talk to him yet. She supposed when she did answer him it would be to say "Yes." Then they would be engaged, and engaged people always seemed silent and dull. She wished he had not spoken so soon. She felt rather afraid of him now, and all their delightful flirtation was at an end. Engaged people never flirted, except with other people, and this kept one or the other of the engaged couple always in a bad temper. She wondered if engagements always seemed so dull. Her mother would be disappointed if she refused him; and why should she say no? There was really no reason that she could think of. Her deep reverie made her forget her breakfast, and everything about her; and as one of the side doors opened she started nervously and came to herself.

A tall, graceful woman entered the room, wearing a trailing dress of some soft, black material. Emily had never seen her before, but she did not seem to be a stranger to the ways of the house. Her beautiful wavy hair was perfectly white, and her complexion colorless; but still she did not look in the least old. Her large, melancholy, black eyes rested for a moment on Emily, and then she took a chair opposite her.

"The ball was a great success last night, was it not, Miss Frankland?"

"Yes, it was delightful. Was madame there? I do not remember seeing her," Emily answered, wondering who this lady with such deep, searching eyes could be, and how she had found out her name.

"No, I was not there. I only arrived last night. I walked a little outside on the terrace, and saw much of the brilliant scene. But I never do more than look on. I resigned my place in society many a long year ago."

"That seems a great pity, if madame enjoys such entertainments."

"But I do not enjoy them, child. I saw you, and enjoyed watching and admiring you. I had curiosity to know who you were, so I asked, and by that means learned your name."

"Perhaps madame would have come to the ball if she had not been alone and among strangers?"

"I am not alone, dear; and this place is one of my homes,— though a very sad one. I am Madame de Lemanski. Perhaps you have heard of my unfortunate son, and will know why I am here?"

"Oh, are you his mother? Then you are not a stranger to me any longer. I do know Count Lemanski, and I have so often wanted to see his mother, and talk to her about his case, which seems so hopeful. He must have greatly improved during this summer?"

"You are very kind to say so, my dear child; and I thank you for speaking so well of my son. But I know from bitter experience that these slight changes for the better count for nothing in the end. No remedy that has yet been tried has ever done him any permanent good. I have given up hope."

"But his case cannot be hopeless when he is so reasonable for days together, each day seeming an improvement on the last."

"But my poor boy has seemed almost recovered countless times before. He always falls back again, as you probably know he has done now. This will go on to the close of his melancholy life."

"Oh, do not say that, Madame de Lemanski. I

know he is worse now,—but it may be such a very long time before his intellect leaves him again."

"I wonder at myself for talking about my afflicted son to strangers. I usually avoid the subject as much as possible. But you seem to invite my confidence. Miss Frankland, will you tell me your first name, and allow me to call you by it? I am sure you have a pretty name."

"Do call me Emily. I shall feel very much pleased and flattered, if you will."

"Thank you, Emily. I hope you will not think me a foolish old woman who is not able to keep her griefs to herself. But my visits here are usually so lonely and wretched. Talking sometimes with a bright young creature, like you, would cheer and comfort me more than anything else."

"I am afraid you will be disappointed in me, Madame de Lemanski; but I shall be delighted if I can be of any use to you. You must know my mother too."

"Thank you, dear. I should like to know Mrs. Frankland; but you must not ask me to go among your gay friends at the hotel. We should not suit each other."

"Will you take walks with me sometimes, madame? That would do you good, I am sure."

"I should like that. Don't, please, talk to me about what my son has been, when you have seen him. I know so well all that, and it tortures me to think of all the rare qualities his irremediable curse of madness obscures."

Emily, in spite of the interest this sad-faced woman inspired, felt rather frightened at the responsibility her patronage seemed to impose.

Madame de Lemanski continued: "I have brought two men with me to take charge of my son Victor. His present attendants are going away,—one is to be married, the other is ill. I have to initiate these men this morning into their duties toward my poor boy, and see if they are competent to occupy the position. It is a difficult charge sometimes. Victor has wonderful cunning about eluding restraint when he has one of his violent attacks. But you have finished your breakfast long ago, Emily, and I am keeping you away from the fresh air, that you need after last night's revels. Go out under the trees, and I will find you there when I have spoken to my men."

Emily went out, and sat in a little arbor, overgrown with wild honeysuckle, to wait for Madame de Lemanski. She chose this concealment because she had no wish to be discovered by any one else. Madame de Lemanski returned in about twenty minutes.

"Emily, *ma petite, où êtes-vous, donc?*" she called.

"*Me voici,* madame!" she answered, coming out of the arbor, with a spray of honeysuckle twined in her hair.

"How pretty you look, child! Come, we will sit under this tree,—there are beetles and earwigs in that arbor; we find more harmless insects in the grass."

While the two ladies engage in another conversation we will leave them, and glance at what is happening in another part of the hotel.

There was a subdued movement and bustle going on in the little flat occupied by the lunatic, Victor de Lemanski. The two keepers who were to leave were putting the rooms in order for their successors. As their patient seemed very quiet and composed on this (to them) eventful morning, they allowed him to go down and sit in the little court-yard. He found engrossing amusement there in wiping the dust off the ivy-leaves with his fine cambric pocket-handkerchief. As this mode of cleaning would afford steady employment for weeks, the men felt safe in leaving their charge alone for an hour. So, after seeing that both entrances to the court were securely fastened on the outside, they went back to their work in the rooms. When this was finished they proceeded to Madame de

Lemanski's room, where they were closeted with her and the two new servants for half an hour, giving and receiving directions.

So the quiet little court was deserted, except by its one industrious tenant. He went on polishing the leaves till his quick ear caught the faint click of a latch behind him. He turned round and listened, and presently the side door was pushed softly open, and a little blue-eyed girl, dressed in white, peered cautiously in, and then started back, frightened at seeing the object of her visit down in the court. But he was too quick for her, and before she could close the door he seized her hand and drew her inside. His manner seemed gentle and kind, so Vera felt no more than a momentary alarm.

"Where are your wings?" he asked, putting his hand on her shoulder, and speaking in French.

"I haven't any," answered Vera, instinctively trying to get a view of her own back.

"Can you walk on two legs if I lead you by one paw? No one shall tread on your tail."

"I can walk on my legs; I am not a baby."

"Come, then. What long fur you have!" he went on, passing his thin fingers through her hair. "You must be an Angora kitten. Go on, we will take a walk," he said, leading her out of the door and

through the little dark passage. As it was the dinner
hour of the men and stable-boys, when Vera and
her crazy companion emerged into the stable-yard
there was no one there to notice or molest them, so
they passed undisturbed under the stone archway,
and from thence into an open field, thickly studded
with trees. Vera was content to wander as far as he
chose, so long as he kept her amused with a string of
nonsensical stories told in a quiet voice. She talked
to him without restraint, feeling as safe with him as
she would have felt with any other of the numerous
gentlemen of her acquaintance, and certainly there
was nothing then in the conduct of the poor lunatic
that could occasion alarm.

In talking to Madame de Lemanski under the trees,
Emily lost a great deal of the shy fear of her that she
had felt while they were in the dining-room, and was
chatting gaily about all the different people she had
met in the last few weeks, when she stopped suddenly
at seeing an expression of alarm pass over Madame
de Lemanski's face. A servant was coming toward
them looking much troubled, and both ladies felt
instinctively that he was the bearer of bad news,
although neither expressed this to the other.

"Ah, *mon Dieu*, what has happened!" exclaimed

Madame de Lemanski, before the man had opened his lips.

He bowed respectfully, and said something in a low tone to Madame de Lemanski.

"Good God! Victor has escaped and cannot be found!" she cried, flying toward the house with a speed that Emily found hard to follow. Then followed an excited investigation of what had happened. After the dismissal of the old guardians, and before the new ones had been installed, the lunatic, by some mismanagement, had been left too long alone. The small door of the court had been opened from the outside in some mysterious way, but minute questioning gave no clue as to how it had been done, and no further trace could be discovered than that he had escaped by this door. A band of men was sent immediately out in pursuit, and there was much running to and fro and gossiping among the servants as to what fate might have befallen the poor runaway. Emily was in Madame de Lemanski's room, doing her best to soothe her heart-rending anxiety.

"Madame, why is it so very dreadful that your son has broken loose for a little while? I should not think it would be alarming,— he wanders about by himself so much when he is well."

"But I have bitter reason to dread his wandering off alone when his brain is all on fire, as it is now. He has twice tried to take his own life at such times. Once he was brought back to me almost drowned,—and the other time,—oh, it is too horrible to tell about! When will this misery end? Go down, Emily dear, and find out if anything has been seen or heard of my poor unfortunate boy. Do not let this oppress your sympathetic little soul,—remember it is only my trouble."

Emily went downstairs with a heavy heart, for she had very little hope of bringing back good news. She walked slowly along one of the avenues, and there encountered the two men who had been engaged to take charge of Count Lemanski. She recognized them, from having seen them a few minutes before in Madame de Lemanski's room, where they had been for further instructions.

"Are you trying to find the poor young gentleman?" she asked of one of them.

"We should be very glad to join in the search," he answered; "but mademoiselle will have the kind-ness to consider that we have not yet seen Monsieur le Comte, whom we are to attend; and even if we knew in what part of the grounds to search, we might not recognize monsieur, if we were so fortunate as to see him."

"I think you would from the description you had from Madame de Lemanski. The best advice I can give you is to continue down this avenue. You have more chance of finding Monsieur le Comte further away from the hotel."

"Mademoiselle is very amiable,—we will obey her."

As the men went on as she had directed, Emily turned to go back to Madame de Lemanski, but as she saw Mr. Haskett coming down the hotel steps she changed her mind, and slipped out of sight behind the trees. She could not see him now. She had not thought of him since breakfast, and she did not want him to discover that her mind was full of Count Lemanski, to the exclusion of himself and his question. He must see this if he spoke to her, so she resolved to avoid him till she felt calmer. She had not told him what time to-day she would give him his answer, and if she spoke to him this evening it would be all that was necessary. She saw, to her great satisfaction, that he did not seem inclined to loiter about the place, but walked briskly toward the main road, down which he soon disappeared.

Emily disliked to go back to Madame de Lemanski with no news of any kind, so, after hesitating a moment, she again walked down the avenue, following in the footsteps of the two guardians.

While these events were transpiring at the *Hôtel des Salines*, Lawrence Conway was on his way back from Saxon. When he went to the station at that place to buy his railway ticket to Bex, he found he had only money enough to take him as far as St. Maurice, and from there he must walk home. This did not disconcert him in the least, as it was only an hour's walk, over a pleasant, winding road, smooth and white as a floor, from St. Maurice to Bex. He had his luggage sent on by train, all the way; he would have money to get it when it arrived, and going by rail himself as far as his ticket permitted, he was soon on the quiet, picturesque road that led to his temporary home. As he walked along he found himself wondering what the people at the hotel were doing. How had Miss Frankland looked at the ball, and had Haskett been dancing attendance on her, as usual? He thought he had grown indifferent about her of late, but now, as he was drawing near where he would soon see her, he felt that all of his old feelings toward her were waking up again. Would she be glad to see him? What would she say? Would she look as lovely as ever, with flowers in her hair? Perhaps the capricious little soul had at last grown tired of Haskett and was ready to cast him off, and welcome him

(Lawrence) back with one of the old sweet smiles she used to give him before Haskett made himself so obtrusive.

Lawrence feared he was not going to be any stronger to resist the charms of this syren than he had been before; — but fate willed that he returned, perhaps fate had some favor in store for him, and he might some day thank the kind friend who had picked his pocket, and driven him back to Bex.

After a walk of three quarters of an hour Lawrence left the main road, and turned into a side path, which presently led to a huge, wide-spreading chestnut tree, marking the beginning of the grounds that belonged to the *Hôtel des Salines*. There was a soft, mossy slope underneath, that formed a most inviting seat. If Lawrence had known that this was one of Emily's favorite haunts, he would not have sat there in the matter-of-fact way that he did, wiping the dust off his boots. He was not at his journey's end yet, but the rest of his way lay through the fields, and down a shady walk, where he would find no dust.

In the same field where the chestnut tree grew was a large, oddly shaped rock, with a vigorous little tree growing in a cleft which nearly split the rock in two. It was cool on sunny days, and pro-

tected on windy days, and the view from it was
very fine, so the little seat in front of the rock was
often occupied. A pale, thin young man, with
wild, black eyes and tangled hair, might have been
seen sitting there this morning talking to a little
girl, who watched him with astonishment in her
big, blue eyes, as he put little bunches of field
flowers in all the button-holes of his coat. As they
were sitting there a wretched, lean dog came swiftly
toward them, snuffing hungrily along the ground.
As soon as Count Lemanski caught sight of him
he gave a shriek, and, seizing Vera round the waist,
rushed like the wind toward the chestnut tree,
carrying his companion under his arm as a gentleman carries his umbrella.

"I will save my little white kitten from that
terrible dog!" he cried anxiously.

Vera, frightened almost out of her senses, uttered
shriek after shriek,— the dog slunk timidly out of
sight, and Lawrence, much startled by the continued screaming, sprang to his feet, and saw flying
toward him a very disheveled looking young man.
One arm was clasped tightly around a heap of short
white petticoats, from the midst of which appeared
a small pair of legs, kicking wildly.

As she was held upside down, Lawrence could

not see the little tear-stained face, half hidden by
long hair, but he recognized the little white shoes
in an instant, and angrily clutching the strange
young man by the arm, released Vera from her in-
verted position, and laid her on the bank. Lawrence's touch reassured her directly, and her loud
crying soon relapsed into an occasional sob.

"What do you mean by frightening that little
girl?" he said, eyeing the Count fiercely.

"*Plait-il?*" he answered. "What little girl?"

"Will you tell me what you mean? Are you
crazy?" Lawrence cried, laying a heavy hand on
the maniac's shoulder.

"He is crazy, Mr. Conway. I did want to tell you
about him, but Mr. Haskett said me not. He live in
a little high room at the hotel; he ought to be take
back."

While Vera was speaking, the Count had quietly
picked up a little twig that was lying on the ground,
and when Lawrence next opened his mouth to speak,
the Count forced the twig suddenly between his
teeth.

"A horse must be kept in with bit and bridle,"
he said, bursting into a childish laugh, as Lawrence
angrily tore away the bit of wood.

"His wits are clean gone. What shall I do with

him!" Lawrence exclaimed. "Vera, can you walk back? It will use all my strength to get this young man home," he said in a whisper to the child.

"I rather walk than be carried under a arm."

"You must be brave, and not get tired," Lawrence answered, grasping the Count's arm firmly, and preparing to lead him back to the hotel. As he turned, the lunatic made another swoop at Vera, but she escaped him by throwing herself flat on the grass before he could catch her.

"No, you must not touch that child again," Lawrence said angrily, trying to drag his captive along faster.

The Count walked along quietly for a short distance, muttering under his breath, "*Voleur! vipère! scélérat!* why did you cross my path?" and then, without any kind of warning, wrenched himself away from Lawrence and sped across the field again. Lawrence pursued him hotly, but as he ran he stumbled over a sharp stone, fell and cut his lip. After a little exercise of profanity, he scrambled to his feet again. But he then saw it was useless to continue the chase; the mad creature ran like a deer, and was almost out of sight already.

"Oh, Mr. Conway, your lip is bleeding! you will soon be a dead. Your hairs is all standing upstairs.

The fault is all to me," wailed Vera, dissolving into tears a second time, and sitting down forlornly in the path.

"Keep your courage up, child; there is nothing to cry about now. We shall be home soon. I must look rather like a madman myself," he said, staunching the blood oozing from his lip—which had already marred the whiteness of his linen—and trying to smooth his ruffled hair with his fingers.

"There are muds on your clothes, too."

"Yes, and I can't brush the *muds* off, either. I hope we shall not meet any one on our way home,—but that would be too much good luck. Come, Vera, I will carry you the rest of the way; you must be very tired."

"You will not carry me as did the other gentleman — wrong side out?"

"No, I am not such a barbarian," Lawrence answered, as he picked up the little girl, and started toward the shady walk that led to the hotel.

CHAPTER XIII.

IN WHICH MR. CONWAY LOSES HIS PATIENCE, TOGETHER WITH HIS LIBERTY.

VERA'S fright and fatigue were telling on her now, and she fell asleep on Lawrence's shoulder, as he hurried along toward the hotel. He quickened his pace as he entered the avenue, and almost ran over two men who were coming the opposite way. He noticed that they looked at him very keenly, but that was only to be expected, considering his disordered dress. He would have wondered if he had seen them stop and look after him, seeming to hesitate whether to follow him or not. Another turn in the avenue, and he came full on Miss Frankland. He knew the plight he was in, and she was the person, above all others, whom he least wished to encounter. But there was no escape; she had seen him, and he could not dart off through the trees, as he had at first thought of doing,— he must meet her, and make some laughing explanation of his appearance, and afterward he could go into particulars.

But as soon as Miss Frankland recognized him, and saw his bleeding face and disordered clothes and hair, she started back with a sharp scream.

"Guards, here is your prisoner; come back!" she shrieked to the two men, who came flying at her call. "Seize him! he is doing his best to escape again! How wild he looks!"

"What does all this mean!" Lawrence exclaimed, putting down the sleepy little girl, and shaking off the hand one of the men had laid on his arm.

"Hold him, both of you," Emily continued angrily. "You seem to be afraid of him!"

"What has everybody the matter with him?" asked sleepy Vera, looking at the excited group in bewilderment.

"Nothing is the matter, Vera. Come with me; we will go back together, and leave these people to follow," Emily said, taking the little girl's hand in hers. "Did the young man hurt you?"

"He carry me upside backward. I was very much *dérangée*, but not hurted."

Emily continued to the two men: "Do not use any more violence than is necessary with the gentleman, but you must bring him back to the hotel, no matter how much resistance he makes. You will be discharged directly if you let him escape again. I will go and tell madame that he has been found. Come, Vera."

"They will not do hurt to my friend, Miss Emily? He has been good."

"No, child, of course they will not hurt him," Emily answered, hurrying away with the little girl.

"Come, now, monsieur," said the elder of the two men, in very good English, trying to push Lawrence along by the shoulder, "it is better not to make any resistance."

"Will you two fellows stop this foolery, and go off about your business!" cried Lawrence, furious at the detention.

"Speak to him in French," said the younger man; perhaps he don't speak English as much as they said he did."

The first man tried addressing him in the language suggested.

"You needn't try to explain yourself in French,— I don't understand it. In plain English, will you instantly release my arm, and let me go?"

"Monsieur cannot escape. I am obliged to answer, No."

"Then take the consequences!" exclaimed Lawrence, giving him a blow in the chest that stretched him on the ground.

This was the signal for violence on the part of the two men. The elder one, who had been knocked down, sprang to his feet instantly, unhurt, and the two together seized Lawrence, forced him down on his knees, and by a great effort succeeded in tying his hands behind him with a heavy silk handkerchief. Lawrence struggled manfully, but the odds were strongly against him. The two men could have mastered him, even when he had all his strength, but this morning he was tired with his previous exertions. At last he gave up, and acknowledged himself beaten, and could only walk quietly back to the hotel, in the hope of getting satisfaction there.

None of the three men were hurt, but their clothes, covered with the soft clay in the path, and Lawrence's bleeding lip, bore unmistakable evidences of a struggle.

"What is the matter? Who is hurt?" asked a dozen voices, as the trio went in at a side-door of the hotel. The men were anxious to escape observation, and bring their prisoner home as quietly as possible, as they had been instructed to do, and they were impatient at the hubbub which ensued among the servants, for it was only some of the underlings of the establishment that they encountered in that part of the house.

"Be quiet, will you! and don't be foolish enough to alarm madame and the whole house. Show us a room with a good lock, where we can deposit monsieur in safety. Be quick, don't stand staring like a set of owls."

There was much subdued questioning and wondering among those of the servants who recognized Lawrence; but alas! all their surmises were made in French, and Lawrence could not relieve his mind here. The door of a small sitting-room was presently opened, and Lawrence was escorted in, too tired now to make any more resistance.

"If monsieur will content himself to wait quietly here, madame his mother will soon visit him."

"Will she? I shall be delighted to see her. In the meantime you will please request Mr. Haskett, an English gentleman, who is here, to come to me. I have something to say to him. Do you hear?"

"I will endeavor to please monsieur," answered the elder of the keepers, bowing himself out and locking the door behind him.

When Lawrence heard the key turn in the lock he first began to realize his position. During the excitement of the past half hour he had been so intent on defending Vera and himself that he had no time to think what was the cause of all the disturbance.

Now he was a prisoner; he had been dragged in the
mud, insulted, overpowered and bound by two ruf-
fians, and exposed like a thief to the impertinent curiosity of the servants. And who had been the cause
of his present humiliation? No one else than the
girl he had been fool enough to admire, and in whose
insanity he had tried not to believe. If it had not
been for her those men in the avenue would never
have given him a moment's thought, and it was only
by her threats and commands that they had been
frightened into making the attack. "Who could
they have been looking for, that she called their
prisoner? It could not have been the poor crazy fellow I met in the field? The men seemed to take me
for some criminal. They are evidently new to the
place, and thought that girl was a responsible person.
But, crazy or wise, Miss Frankland has gone too far
this time. She or her mother shall give me an explanation of what has happened, and I *will* get satisfaction for this scandalous treatment in some way.
This makes the second time this bewitched girl has
attacked me. When I was helping Vera out of a
scrape, the first occasion, by the lake, was rather
amusing, but this last escapade has no semblance of a
joke."

At this juncture a servant came in bearing a tray

with luncheon. Lawrence tried to question the man as to how long his imprisonment was to last, but could gather nothing from him except that somebody was coming some time. He was carefully locked in again, and after his lunch, which he found very refreshing, he stretched himself on the sofa, where, his weary members getting the better of his agitated thoughts, he soon fell into a sound sleep.

Emily, returning to the house with Vera, found the little girl too tired and worn out to give anything but a very confused account of what had happened; so she left off questioning her, and gave her in charge of Annette as soon as possible. Emily then went to find Madame de Lemanski, to tell her that the wanderer was found.

"You are a dear, good child, to bring me such welcome news!" that lady exclaimed, kissing Emily on both cheeks affectionately.

"I think, madame, it will be well to wait until he has grown calm before you visit him. I was told that he had stopped his complaints and was not so restless as at first. They are going to take him something to eat, and if you would go in to see him in the course of the afternoon you might find him quite rational. That would be such a consolation to you."

"I will follow your advice, Emily. I think I will try to sleep for an hour; I am in sore need of it. You are sure my boy is as comfortable as possible?"

"Oh yes, madame. You need not have any anxiety about that; he is in a very pleasant little room, and there is a servant stationed within hearing to go to him if he calls. I will leave you now, madame, and you must take a refreshing sleep; there is nothing to be troubled about any more."

Emily felt much exhausted herself, and as she was about to throw herself on her own bed to rest she caught sight of a letter on her dressing-table. The contents were as follows:

My Dear Miss Emily,—A telegram received this morning requests my presence at Aigle, to see, on business, a friend of my mother's, who is stopping at that place for two days. Much as it costs me to cause the delay of the answer I hoped to hear to-day, I cannot avoid being absent from Bex till to-morrow.

Hoping you are feeling no over fatigue from the ball, I am Yours most sincerely,
Sidney Gore Haskett.
Hôtel des Salines, Friday morning.

This letter was a great relief to Emily, for it gave her plenty of time to calm herself and collect her ideas before the interview with the man who had asked her to be his wife. She was glad of the chance to be able to rest, with no more disturbing thoughts

for that day at least. At the suggestion of Mrs.
Frankland the two ladies dined alone, and as the fine
day had ended with a gloomy, drizzling rain, neither
Emily nor her mother appeared downstairs again that
evening. Emily thought it more discreet not to visit
Madame de Lemanski again till that lady sent for
her; so arraying herself in a pretty dressing-gown,
of some soft, blue stuff, she made herself as comfortable as possible on the sofa, to read, think, or fall
asleep.

It was late in the afternoon when Lawrence awoke
refreshed from his nap; and with the awakening came
a determination to put an end to his irritating bondage. He went to the window and tried to open it,
with the intent either to climb out or call till some
one came to his rescue, whom he could make understand what was the matter. He had just made the
unpleasant discovery that the window was fastened
tightly down when he heard the door of his prison
unlocked for the second time.

A tall, white-haired lady, with mournful black
eyes, glided swiftly toward him and threw her arms
around his neck:

"My own dear boy, do you know your mother?"
she said, with much emotion, turning his face to the
light——

"O *mon Dieu!* who are you? You are not my son — how came you here?" she exclaimed, pushing him away from her and starting back.

"Madame, I shall be most delighted to answer your questions; you are the first person who has been kind enough to give me a hearing to-day. My name is Lawrence Conway. I have not the honor to be your son, and I came here through the caprice or malice — I am unable say which — of a young lady, Miss Emily Frankland by name, and I have to thank her for the very disagreeable attack and imprisonment to which I have been subjected to-day."

"Miss Frankland? Yes, I know. She told me I should find here my son, Victor de Lemanski. There has been some grave mistake. I am utterly unable to account for it."

"Madame, it is the simplest thing in the world to account for what has happened. Since her arrival here Miss Frankland has persistently called me Count Lemanski, which I now learn to be the name of your son. At first, I tried to persuade her that she was mistaken, but I soon discovered that it was not a mistake, but a mania, on her part, to cherish strange delusions about people, and that she was unfortunately responsible for very little that she said or did. I have long suspected that such a gentleman as

Count Lemanski existed, and that Miss Frankland,
either because of her distorted imagination, or to
please a passing whim, bestowed his name on me.
When inquiries were made about your son — (I infer
that there must have been some alarm or disturbance early this morning) — Miss Frankland settled
on me as the person desired. I was taken into
custody, and here I have been ever since. Most of
the mystery is now clear to me. I am very sorry
that you have been disappointed, madame. If you
had been here longer, you would have learned not
to trust to anything Miss Frankland said."

"What you say astonishes me more and more,
Mr. Conway. I have been struck with admiration
of Miss Frankland's character during the short
time I have known her, and have not noticed the
slightest tinge of any of the peculiarities you have
mentioned. I cannot help thinking your judgment
harsh and severe in' the extreme. It cannot be
more than a grave mistake that has caused your
arrest to-day. I will do my best to discover the
error, and that will be the best way to express my
profound regret for the indignity you have been
made to suffer. A bare apology seems inadequate to
atone for the discomfort you have undergone."

"Madame, I beg of you to say nothing more about

apology. You are perfectly innocent of all blame, and in at last liberating me you are doing me the greatest favor possible. Let us leave this room, my associations with it are very unpleasant."

"You will excuse me, Mr. Conway, if I tell you nothing about my poor son now; it is a heart-rending subject. Some other time I will tell you his history, Tor an explanation is due to you, beyond all doubt. Oh my God, I had forgotten my unfortunate boy; he is still wandering alone and unprotected! Come, Mr. Conway, your sufferings are over; mine, alas! are only increased."

Lawrence felt much sympathy for the unknown sorrow of this interesting woman, but as long as she withheld her confidence he could do nothing to help her. With a renewed apology for his unpleasant experience that day, Madame de Lemanski left him, and Lawrence, now at liberty, took refuge in his own room.

Madame de Lemanski's curiosity and astonishment at the discovery just made was quite swallowed up in the renewed anxiety she felt in the fate of her son. She hurriedly summoned the band of men who had been recalled from the search, and ordered them out again to follow the fugitive more carefully than before. She could not believe the hard things Mr.

Conway had said about Emily; she was convinced of a great error somewhere, which she would try to right as soon as she felt calmer; now her brain seemed on fire, and she could think of nothing but the possible sufferings of her unhappy son. Toward evening she wrote a few lines to Emily, telling her briefly that the gentleman who had been arrested was not her son, and that her anxiety for Victor was almost insupportable. She would explain everything when Emily came to see her again. This note was intrusted to a boy resplendent in buttons, who deposited it on Miss Frankland's plate at the dinner-table. He had not been instructed to do this, and the letter was not sufficiently addressed to be left to find its own way. As Miss Frankland did not come to dinner, the little note was overlooked and finally picked up off the floor and taken to the bureau. The address, "Miss Emily," was too vague to admit of its being delivered to anyone, so it staid in the office till it lost its power of doing good.

CHAPTER XIV.

MR. CONWAY IS APPEASED.

EMILY was out early the next morning; she had so much to think of that sleep was impossible, and the morning was too beautiful to be wasted indoors.

She rambled off down the avenue, the scene of yesterday's adventures, wondering how Madame de Lemanski had found her son, and a little puzzled that she had not been sent for again. Mr. Haskett was coming home to-day; she wished she knew when, and where she could meet him. She rather hoped he would arrive by one of the late trains. It was a pity that he was so matter-of-fact and cold-blooded; but then he was English — that accounted for it. He would be much more agreeable if he were animated like — Darwin, for instance, when he was well.

Poor Darwin! she was afraid she would not see him any more at his best. He must have been very violent to make all this commotion. It would take him a long time to recover, and she would probably have left the *Salines* before he was better again.

Madame de Lemanski was charming. How very deserving of pity she was! and what ornaments to society the mother and son might be — under different circumstances.

She wandered on, and at last reached the chestnut tree, and sat down on the little bank to continue the train of her thoughts. She went on dreaming till startled by a peculiar grunting screech from the branches of the tree. She looked up quickly, but, seeing nothing, concluded it was a stray magpie, or, perhaps, crows fighting, and thought no more about it. A moment after, a chestnut, in its prickly bur, fell, striking her on the shoulder. Her dress was of thin muslin, and the sensation was very unpleasant. Then another fell, and another, and before Emily could spring to her feet she found herself a target to a volley of chestnut burs, aimed with a directness which no wind could ever accomplish; besides, it was a very calm day, and there was scarcely any breeze stirring.

Emily looked up again, thoroughly alarmed, and saw a pair of long legs dangling from the tree, apparently in search of a resting-point from which to jump There was nothing unusual in these legs, decorously arrayed in black broadcloth, it was only their unexpected appearance in that elevated place that frightened Emily. The next moment, a pale, dark-eyed, rather handsome young man, whom Emily had never seen before, slid to the ground and stood before her.

His dress was that of a gentleman, but his whole appearance was disordered and wild, especially as he wore no hat, and his long black hair was scattered over his face.

He carried in his hand a stick with a gauze net at one end for entrapping insects, and there were bits of withered flowers hanging in many of his buttonholes.

He stared at Emily till a pleased smile broke over his vacant face, showing to advantage his beautiful white teeth. He then advanced a little nearer, and timidly putting out his hand tried to stroke Emily's uncovered hair as he asked:

"Whose little dog are you?"

Emily put up her hand to ward him off, and stared at him in amazement.

"Monsieur is incomprehensible," she said.

"You are a pretty little white poodle, but cross; do you bite when you are petted?"

"Yes, I am very dangerous." Emily was trembling all over with fright, but still could not help being amused at her strange companion.

"That is because you are hungry. I will find you something to eat."

He walked on a little, to Emily's great relief, and as he rushed at and pinned down with his net every flower that stirred in the breeze, Emily did not know whether to stay and watch his amusing antics or to take refuge in flight.

While he was shrieking and dancing with delight at having imprisoned a nodding spray of foxglove, Emily conquered her curiosity and started for home. The young man was either drunk or mad, and it was dangerous to be alone with him at that distance from the hotel. But when she turned to go, it was as if he had eyes in the back of his head to watch her movements. He rushed after her, and though she was far in advance and ran at the top of her speed, her flight was suddenly stopped by her pursuer clapping the butterfly trap over her head like an extinguisher, with which he led her backward to the tree. Emily was now frightened beyond all control. She gave one long, shrill scream for help, but no answer came, and her terror seemed to excite her assailant to more violence than he had already shown. He clutched at the knot of curls hanging down her back, saying:

"If you will sit quietly under the tree, my little dog, I will find you something nice to eat. If you howl and whine, I will cut off your curls and throw stones at you. It is better to obey."

Emily remembered that at about this time in the
morning two children usually came along the avenue,
carrying milk to the hotel. She would be as calm as
possible till they or some one else came. Her only
deliverance lay in this, for she never could save herself by running from her swift-footed oppressor. If
Mr. Haskett would only come!—she would never
call him cold-blooded or slow again. White as a
ghost, she sat down on the bank and watched, with
a gloomy fascination, her captor, as he peered into
the grass and stirred up the dead leaves.

The morning after his arrest and imprisonment
Lawrence felt less resentment, but his curiosity was
redoubled. In the coffee-room he met the Countess
de Lemanski, who, after they had breakfasted, proposed a walk in the grounds, where she could give
him a further explanation of the events of the
evening before. Lawrence, nothing loath, accepted,
and, as they turned into the avenue, he was prepared to listen intently to the subject uppermost in
the minds of both, when a sound in the distance
attracted his attention.

"I thought I heard a scream; did you notice anything, madame?"

"No, I heard nothing."

"It was only my imagination, I suppose. This

avenue, and the field beyond, are now associated in my mind with shrieks and struggles."

"I wish we could all forget that unfortunate affair of yesterday, Mr. Conway. It preys on my mind more than I can express. I wonder that child Emily has not been to talk to me about it: she must have received the note I sent last night."

"Forgetfulness is another of Miss Frankland's failings, Madame de Lemanski."

"You are too hard on this young lady, Mr. Conway. I am going to try to make you understand each other, for I am sure you cannot have done so before. Her maid told me she had walked down this avenue. I hope we may meet her, and then she will make such a pretty apology for her mistake, that you will have to forgive her. How lovely this morning is!"

"It is charming. I am delighted to see you so well and cheerful, Madame de Lemanski."

"That is because I have had what I call good news to-day."

"Indeed! I am happy to hear it."

"I heard, this morning, from a cottager of the neighborhood, that my poor son, whom I had imagined wandering without shelter all night, had supped and lodged in his cottage, and had left it early this morning; so I have every hope that he will be found to-day."

"This must be a great weight off your mind, madame."

"Oh, indeed it is! And I feel that I must do all in my power to amend what you and Miss Emily have suffered because of my son,—for I am sure she is very unhappy in knowing what her mistake has occasioned. There is much about the whole affair that I do not understand: when we meet her, we will have a clear explanation."

"There certainly is some disturbance going on ahead of us, Madame de Lemanski. Could you walk a little faster, or shall I go on ahead, and see what is the trouble?"

"I do hear something like a person crying or calling for help. Do let us make haste! I can go very fast when I am excited. Can it be my boy in trouble? Oh, Mr. Conway, I am so glad you are with me!"

"Do not be frightened, madame, it may be nothing. The sound comes from the field ahead of us; I see nothing yet. I am afraid you are exerting yourself too much, madame. You are walking faster than I can."

After searching carefully among the leaves for a few minutes, Emily's companion discovered a small brown lizard, which he pursued and finally caught in his net. He then took it out of the net, and dangled it before

Emily, holding it between his finger and thumb, say-ing, in a coaxing tone, "Puppies like nice fat lizards; eat it, little dog, I am sure you are hungry."

Emily shrank back in disgust at the slimy, squirm-ing creature held so close before her eyes.

"Bark, first, and then you shall have it. Bark! I tell you. Do you hear!" he cried, seizing her rough-ly by the arm, and holding the lizard so close that it almost touched her cheek. She screamed again and again, and tried to escape, but it seemed hopeless. The now enraged lunatic caught her round the neck, and with the other hand held the writhing reptile to her lips, crying, "Eat it, then, without barking! Be quick, or it will get away, and my trouble will go for nothing."

Emily, her whole face transfigured with horror and loathing, slipped on to her knees, and tried to pro-pitiate her persecutor with her tearful entreaties. Suddenly he loosened his grasp, the lizard slid from his hands, and Emily felt herself free. The lunatic was staring at two persons who were hurrying to-ward them,— one was a tall lady with gray hair, the other an excited-looking young gentleman, who called angrily:

"Hands off, you ruffian! How dare you frighten that young lady?"

"Thank heavens! here is help at last," sighed Emily, as she threw herself into the outstretched arms of Madame de Lemanski. But that lady soon put her gently aside, and glided over to the poor lunatic, who was standing motionless, with his head fallen on his breast.

"My son, Victor, do you not know your own loving mother?" she said in a soft, low voice, taking his face in both her hands, and looking steadily in his eyes. The young man burst into tears, and sank down on the grass.

"He will be better now," said the white-haired lady, with a smile of subdued happiness. "Mr. Conway, Emily, congratulate me; I have found my son."

"Then you had two missing sons, madame?" asked Emily, in astonishment."

"No, my dear, Mr. Conway is not my son. You have been mistaken all along."

"Mr. Conway? This gentleman is Count Lemanski, and not your son! I do not understand."

"I have frequently told Miss Frankland that my name was not Lemanski, but she never chose to believe it," said Lawrence, dryly.

"Madame, do you tell me that this gentleman's name is Conway, and that he is not your insane son?"

"I do, mademoiselle, emphatically. Who can have been your false informant?"

"Then it must be true. Mr. Conway, I have been putting myself and you in a most perplexing light for weeks. Will you have the patience to come back to the hotel with me, and listen to a long explanation,— for I can see how the mistake has been carried on now, from beginning to end. It was all my fault."

At first Lawrence listened with indifference to all that Miss Frankland said, but presently, for the first time in many days, he began to think that she spoke the truth. As she proceeded, a flush of pleasure mounted to his cheek at the thought that the mystery of the past few weeks was soon to be so satisfactorily solved; and by the time they reached the hotel all was explained.

While Madame de Lemanski led her now submissive son to his own apartments, Emily and Lawrence went to the *salon*, where Emily began the long story over again from the point of Winnie's departure; and the two young people, who were now so happily reconciled to each other, had many a quiet laugh over the host of absurd situations Winnie's innocent words had caused. Everything was made clear but the conduct of Mr. Haskett.

"It seems as if he had been playing traitor," Lawrence mused.

"He has deceived me hundreds of times——"

Emily stopped short as she remembered that she was speaking of the man whose wife she soon would pledge herself to be.

"But we must not condemn him unheard," continued Lawrence. "Perhaps he can prove his innocence."

"I cannot see what object he could have had for deceiving me."

Lawrence was like a different man that evening, as he sat at dinner talking to his fair neighbor without restraint, and he felt that he should never cease to congratulate himself that he had lost his money at Saxon. This loss had brightened the whole world to him, and he felt overflowing with a new, keen happiness. Mr. Haskett returned that same evening, but too late to make his arrival known to any of the persons in whom he was most interested.

CHAPTER XV.

CONCLUSION.

MR. HASKETT felt his face change color as he strolled into one of the little reception rooms after breakfast the next morning and saw the group assembled there. Mrs. Frankland was sitting on the sofa talking gayly to Lawrence Conway, who was engaged in searching through a pile of music on the table. Emily was at the piano, with one pretty hand resting on the keys. Her face was turned toward Lawrence, on whom she was venting occasional playful sarcasms for being so long in finding the music he wanted.

Mr. Haskett saw instantly, from the expression of their faces, that things were not as they had been. What evil fate had brought that fellow Conway back so soon, just as he felt so sure of his game? Mr. Haskett's first impulse was to turn and keep out of sight till he had arranged a plan of defense, for he felt beyond a doubt that defense would be necessary; but it was too late to retreat.

"Oh, there is Mr. Haskett!" Emily exclaimed, rising and coming forward.

"I have come for my answer, Emily," he said in a low tone, as he nervously pressed her hand.

"But you must answer some questions first!" she rejoined gayly. "You are to be our prisoner till you have given us a clear explanation of what has been puzzling us for so long."

"Good morning, Mrs. Frankland. Do you wonder if I feel overwhelmed with the importance of the task your daughter has imposed on me?"

"We all look to you for light in this matter, Mr. Haskett. I hope you will not disappoint us."

Mr. Haskett wished devoutly that he was a star of lesser magnitude on this occasion.

"How are you, Conway?" he asked, with an assumption of indifference. "I did not expect to see you here again so soon."

"I am happy to say that circumstances obliged me to return sooner than I intended, thereby enabling me to clear up a misunderstanding that has been allowed to exist for weeks. Mr. Haskett, will you please explain why you permitted me to suppose that Miss Frankland was insane, when you knew the contrary; and why you did not break up that young lady's delusion about me, when you, and you only, had the power to do away with a mistake that was causing endless perplexities to people whom you were pleased to call your friends?"

'So, my dear fellow, you have discovered this little joke at last! I knew it must come out soon. It was making such a capital story — quite like the absurd situations one reads about, you know — that I hated to break it all up by letting in the light of common-sense. I hope you are not going to take it seriously?"

"You knew all the time that we were mistaken in each other — Mr. Conway and I?" Emily asked, wonderingly, as she looked from Mr. Haskett to Lawrence.

"How curious that you should have cared to keep the secret so long," Mrs. Frankland mused.

Mr. Haskett smiled feebly as he finished speaking, but he saw no reflection of his smile on Lawrence's face.

"And so you deliberately let two people suffer untold annoyance and anxiety for weeks simply for the sake of carrying on what you chose to call an amusing joke? Mr. Haskett, you have had a deeper motive. Will you favor me with the *truth*, where we can talk to each other undisturbed? This is no place for the words I have still to say to you."

"If the conversation you purpose to favor me with is to be as insulting as your last words have been, I agree with you that it cannot continue in the presence of ladies. I will see you in your room, an hour from now," answered Mr. Haskett, hotly.

"Gentlemen, I beg of you not to take this affair so seriously!" cried Mrs. Frankland nervously.

"Do not excite yourself, Mrs. Frankland; there is no cause for uneasiness."

"I will wait for you in my room at twelve o'clock, Mr. Haskett," Lawrence said, as, with a graceful bow to the two ladies, he stepped through the long window out on to the lawn. Mrs. Frankland followed him, with a vague idea of calming his troubled thoughts, and Emily and Mr. Haskett were left alone.

During the interval of silence, Vera, tired and flushed with the exertion of trying to teach her little brother to dance to the music of her bottle, before he knew how to walk, came and stretched herself across the window-sill. She leaned her golden head on a velvet footstool on the mosaic floor, and, with her little white feet resting on the grass outside, she fell asleep, with her musical bottle under one arm. She saw neither of the occupants of the room, and was so quiet that they scarcely noticed her.

At length Mr. Haskett crossed the room to where Emily was sitting, and, with his voice trembling with emotion, said, taking her hand in his:

"Miss Frankland — Emily — you will not let what you have to tell me be influenced by what this hot-headed fellow has just said?"

"But, Mr. Haskett, I cannot help feeling amazed that you could carry on such a deception toward a man you have always called your friend!"

"Perhaps I was wrong in speaking of him as my friend; he is nothing more than a chance acquaintance. I fail to see why I am bound to make myself responsible for the wrong ideas of other people that he chooses to take into his head. If he was fool enough to doubt your intelligence, was I obliged to labor with him till he changed his mind? He ought to blame himself, and no one else, for what was caused by his own stupidity. It is the height of impertinence for him to make me so conspicuous in the affair."

"But why did you let me believe he was insane, Mr. Haskett? I have made myself so ridiculous in his eyes because of that belief."

"I only knew him as a companion on the mountains; how could I answer for his conduct in polite society? If he impressed you as insane, what proof had I to the contrary? Ever since I have been here my heart and brain have been filled with your image. I have had neither the power nor inclination to study and understand the character of a man to whom I am perfectly indifferent. Oh, Emily, you cannot be so cruel as to dash my happiness to the ground because of this foolish error! Answer me, my darling,— tell me that you will be my wife," he said, fervently pressing both her hands to his lips.

"Don't touch me — let me think," she answered, pushing him gently away, and falling back on the sofa from which she had risen.

Her brain was in a tumult. She felt that there was a ring of falseness through all Mr. Haskett had said. He had been very unjust to Mr. Conway, and she resented this keenly for his sake and for her own. But then it was true that Mr. Haskett was not responsible for the opinions Mr. Conway might form of other people, and should she refuse him for carrying his love of joking too far? He would then go away— Mr. Conway also — and she would be left to feel over again the monotony that had hung over the first days of her stay at the hotel. She would probably repent her decision when too late to retract her word; and then her mother would be so disappointed,— she had quite set her heart on Emily's marrying Mr. Haskett.

No, she could not refuse; but then could she accept a man who had been acting a lie to her for weeks? It was a hard question to settle,— and all the time he was devouring her with his eyes, as he stood before her waiting for her reply. Why were there no longer good fairies who could come and inspire her with the words she might say and never repent?

A toddling, staggering baby on the grass outside fell over Vera's legs and woke her up. She sleepily rubbed her eyes and stroked the back of her neck, stiff from the position she had taken on the footstool, then, for diversion, set up her bottle on the floor, and leaned back against the window-frame to listen.

At the other side of the room Emily heard, mingling in with her reverie, the sound of soft, tinkling music. She did not know or care where it came from, but was only aware that it was pleasant and soothing. It was the same air from *"Don Juan"* that she remembered the band played one exquisite afternoon when she wandered so far away with Mr. Conway. How long ago that seemed, and how she had regretted that day that her companion was insane! But he was not insane — did she realize that?

"Emily, have you forgotten me? — or can I take your long silence for consent?" asked a voice so close that she felt its warm breath on her cheek.

The soft melody repeated itself, the words chasing each other in wild confusion through Emily's brain:

" Je voudrais, mais je n'ose,
　　J'espère, et puis j'ai peur;
　C'est le ciel qu'il propose,
　　Mais s'il est un trompeur?"

As the course of a stream is turned by a pebble, Emily felt the words of assent, trembling on her lips, changed and chased away by this tiny echo of familiar music. There was inspiration and warning in every note. She started to her feet, held out her hand, and, looking her lover full in the face, said with a clear, firm voice:

"Mr. Haskett, I beg your pardon for my hesitation. I should have answered you an hour ago. I cannot be your wife. I hope you will not think me unkind, but to the question you asked me on the night of the ball, and repeated to-day, I must answer no."

"But, Miss Frankland, I had hoped for a very different answer. I cannot have understood. You speak hastily. I will give you more time."

"Time will not alter my decision, Mr. Haskett. May I beg of you to accept it as final?"

As soon as Emily uttered the one decisive monosyllable "no," she felt a load removed from her heart and mind that had been almost greater than the could bear. In the careless happiness that pervaded her whole being she felt a proud confidence that she had answered right.

"Miss Frankland, I cannot realize that you mean this cruel answer to be final. I will go away for a week — for a month — if you say so, and then perhaps you will think differently?"

"You would be wiser not to return on my account, Mr. Haskett."

Mr. Haskett broke into one more eloquent appeal to Emily to retract her word or hold out a surer hope than he already had for the future, but she was inexorable; and at last the discarded lover left the room, inwardly cursing the folly of his conduct toward Conway, for he felt it was this that had changed Emily's feelings, and he could not deny that she had justice on her side.

As Mr. Haskett disappeared through the door, Emily went over to the window, caught up Vera and whirled her around the room in a mad, merry dance, in which the little girl's short, bare legs rarely reached to the floor. Then, after chasing each other around and around the table, the two children, tired out with laughing and romping, sat down again on the window-sill.

"Why are you so very much happy, Miss Emily?"

"Because I said to somebody what I thought, Vera."

"I say sometimes so, and get scolds from people, but I think not nice things like you."

"Where did you get your bottle, Vera? Is that what made the music a little while ago?"

"Yes; is he not beautiful?"

Emily pressed her warm, red lips against the unyielding side of the bottle.

"Mr. Conway give him to me; I name him Lawrence for he."

"That is a great honor for Mr. Conway — does he know it?"

"Yes, he know everything. He is coming — see, down there. Mr. Conway! come in and see Miss Emily and me!"

Lawrence heard the little girl's call and stopped outside the window to talk.

"I have waited half an hour longer than the time fixed, in my room, to see Mr. Haskett, but he has not appeared. Do you know what has become of him, Miss Frankland?"

"He left this room about half an hour ago. Further than that I know nothing of him."

"Isn't your bottle demolished yet, Vera?"

"I don't know. When I tell Miss Emily my bottle was named you, she did a kiss on it."

"Why Vera!" Emily exclaimed, blushing hotly, "how shockingly you misrepresent!"

An amused smile crept over Lawrence's face, and though he said nothing he would have given his ears to know what was the real episode of the bottle. What made Miss Frankland blush so? Vera must tell him what it was later.

That evening it was rumored that Mr. Haskett had left the hotel. He had not said where he was going, but he paid his bill and took all his luggage with him; so the departure must have been premeditated and final. There was no note or word of good-bye left for any one, and the members of the hotel were left to account for his absence in whatever way they saw fit. "Cowardly sneak!" was all Mr. Conway was ever heard to remark on the subject of his departure.

At the close of a lovely afternoon in September two persons are idly walking along the shore of the lake. Both are silent, but it is not for lack of ideas, each being in a mood to indulge in what the Germans call the "*stumme sprache*." At last the gentleman speaks:

"The last time I asked you to go over to the island you refused. May I ask you again, Miss Frankland?"

"Yes, let us go out on the water — it is so beautifully clear." They rowed over to the fragrant little island, and there, within hearing of the fitful tones of the harp, Lawrence told Emily the old story which is never worn out. It must have been a long story, for the daylight faded and the stars came twinkling into sight before the plashing of the oars was heard bringing them back to shore.

As they came back to the hotel Vera danced forward to meet them:

"Miss Emily, you look at Mr. Conway like as you thought he was a very good fellow. I am glad ——"

"I do think so, Vera."

"Do you like him so much as I do?"

"As much and more than you ever loved anybody, little girl."

www.ingramcontent.com/pod-product-compliance
Lightning Source LLC
Chambersburg PA
CBHW020604030726
47497CB00007B/2079